PENGUIN BOOKS

ROAR

ROAR

Manjeet Mann

PENGUIN BOOKS

PENGUIN BOOKS

UK | USA | Canada | Ireland | Australia
India | New Zealand | South Africa

Penguin Books is part of the Penguin Random House group of companies whose addresses can be found at global.penguinrandomhouse.com

www.penguin.co.uk
www.puffin.co.uk
www.ladybird.co.uk

First published 2025

001

Text copyright © Manjeet Mann, 2025
Cover illustration copyright © Kushiaania, 2025

The moral right of the author and illustrator has been asserted

The Audre Lorde quote in the epigraph is from *Sister Outsider*, first published in the USA by Crossing Press, 1984, and in Great Britain by Penguin Books, 2019.
Text copyright © Audre Lorde, 1984.

Penguin Random House values and supports copyright. Copyright fuels creativity, encourages diverse voices, promotes freedom of expression and supports a vibrant culture. Thank you for purchasing an authorized edition of this book and for respecting intellectual property laws by not reproducing, scanning or distributing any part of it by any means without permission. You are supporting authors and enabling Penguin Random House to continue to publish books for everyone. No part of this book may be used or reproduced in any manner for the purpose of training artificial intelligence technologies or systems. In accordance with Article 4(3) of the DSM Directive 2019/790, Penguin Random House expressly reserves this work from the text and data mining exception.

Text design by Janene Spencer
Printed in Great Britain by Clays Ltd, Elcograf S.p.A.

The authorized representative in the EEA is Penguin Random House Ireland, Morrison Chambers, 32 Nassau Street, Dublin D02 YH68

A CIP catalogue record for this book is available from the British Library

ISBN: 978-0-241-64762-2

All correspondence to:
Penguin Books
Penguin Random House Children's
One Embassy Gardens, 8 Viaduct Gardens, London SW11 7BW

Penguin Random House is committed to a sustainable future for our business, our readers and our planet. This book is made from Forest Stewardship Council® certified paper.

For the quiet ones

*'Sometimes, we are blessed with being able to choose
the time and the arena and the manner of our revolution,
but more usually,
we must do battle where we are standing.'*

– Audre Lorde

PROLOGUE

The warrior within

In ancient times there were female warriors.
Warriors who led armies into battle,
fought men twice their size
sizing them up on the field
before slaying them
fighting them and frightening them.

These warrior women
rode on the backs of lions.
Sword in hand they
revolted against kings,
gained control of kingdoms
and placed the kingly crowns on their own heads.

These long-forgotten warriors
fought for freedoms
thinking the battle was won
but here we are still fighting
still cycling through rising and falling
folding in on ourselves
trying to shrink ourselves and tell ourselves,

Don't be bright, bold, brave
be small, sexy, smiley.
Be. Nice.

And when some have had enough
we all rise with a hashtag
surfing on clouds.
Finally! We rejoice. We're there.

There where?
When there are girls being banned from school
and married off too soon
and when her body is presented battered and bruised
there are picket lines
stripping her of her right to choose.
It's hard to remember there's a warrior inside us,
when there are TikTok stars
who deserve to be behind bars.
It's hard to see that warrior
but she's there
you've just got to believe it.

Look in the mirror
and you'll see her
staring back at you
saying you don't have to be extraordinary
or have a gift
or a special power
some otherworldly god-like quality
you don't need a sword, a tiger, a boon
you can do extraordinary things and be perfectly
normal.

The warrior is in you.
The hero is in you.
Yes you sitting there one eye on the TV
one eye on your phone double-screening,
she's in you scrolling through socials sitting in a cafe
and you still in bed past noon
and you counting the pennies
and you back from the night shift
and you on the school run

and you clock-watching in maths
and you studying for your next exam
and you back-chatting the teacher
and you being bullied in the corner
and you dealing with anxiety
and you having to grow up before you had to
and you who haven't grown up enough . . . yet
and you
and you
and you.

We're not so different from each other
you over there, her on the other side of the globe.
Deep down we want the same
need the same
love the same.

Over there they have more money
over here more power
more of something
more than you
more than them
more than her on the other side of the globe.

But underneath it
we're all just out here
fighting, living, winning, losing
battling each day
in the only way we know how
the only way we can
from the depths of our stomach
from the heat in our blood
from the fire in our throat

*some silently, some loudly, some unknowingly
roaring for more.*

*So, take courage and listen to the call.
That is the journey of the hero after all.*

*Born into a world not quite fitting in
they search in every corner of their skin
searching for themselves,
swimming through a sea of voices
so confused they don't recognize their own reflection,
so lost that when they hear the call to roar they deny it.
They lock the door and hide behind it
but the call, it doesn't quit, it keeps knocking
until finally the hero, shaking in their boots, opens to a crack of light
and steps out. Frightened and falling
they start on their path, ready for a fight.
The hero builds muscle and gathers an army
they slay dragons and topple gods
until finally
they come face-to-face with themselves
and see themselves.
It's as clear as day.
No more confusion,
no more hiding,
no more swimming through voices.
They take what they know,
the wonder, the secrets, the magic of it all
back to the ordinary world
and show the people they too
can roar for more.
That is the hero's journey after all.*

So . . .

Let's spin the globe now.
Let's meet our hero.
Zoom in, closer, closer, closer
until you see a white mansion sitting in the middle
of a gated community among other white mansions
nestled in an environment of unequivocable exclusivity
in the city of New Delhi.

We begin at the end.
An epic ending to an epic tale.

It's the middle of the night and a young woman
who came into this world with a roar
fists clenched ready for a fight
stands looking at this house
thinking about how she got here
thinking about the people who turned her into a fugitive
thinking about where she'll run next.

She's only seventeen.
An ordinary young woman fighting ordinary people
who have given themselves the title 'god'.
But these so-called gods
did not bank on coming up against
such an extraordinary young woman.
A young woman wielding her own Kali.
A young woman with her tribe of divine women
weapons in hand, tiger on command,
roaming the ravines
slaying dragons, toppling gods
and ready for revenge.

She stands looking at this white mansion.

It's so quiet, she thinks, not a soul in sight.
Crickets providing a soundtrack to the night.
The night hot and sticky,
the air dry, the wind warm.
It's the height of summer
just before the rains.
She thinks about this house,
the house that started it all,
beads of sweat trickling down her temples
hair sticking to her forehead.
She is a world away from the young woman she once was
when she lived behind these gates, gates that protect
this community from people like her.
The person she has now become.

This is our warrior,
our hero and

her
name
is

Rizu.

She smiles at the moon.
It'll be her only witness tonight.
Lingering in the quiet
she draws in a deep breath
lifts her head and

roars.

ONE

Metamorphosis

Come out, come out wherever you are,
I whisper into the night.
My words shake, swallowed by shadows.
Rama purrs, a steady rhythm to my unsteady heart.

What now, Rizu? Annika asks.
Her fingers dancing
a nervous ballet across her lips.

You can turn back if you want, I say.

You shouldn't be alone for this.

I want to tell her
I am best alone, stronger even.
Fine.
We wait for them to leave.

I concentrate on my target as lights dim one by one,
their darkness – my silent cue.
A final command, an enthusiastic goodbye,
one by one they leave the house.

A smile creeps across my lips
as memories flood my mind.
Before the hunt, the chaos,
the tribe, the splintering, the plan.
Before the change.

I look at my reflection in the fountain.
It is a stranger's face now.
Remarkable, unrecognizable,
my metamorphosis –
                      complete.

Look at these self-made gods, Rama.
They think of themselves as invincible
yet their power is a fragile illusion.
Tonight, Rama, their delusion will be crushed.

Rama growls, tension ripples through his muscles.
Annika edges away.
The tiger still startles her.
I stroke his strong, powerful back.
Rama chuffs and licks at my feet.

We wait, watch as the servants leave
on the back of mopeds
thundering their way out of the mansion complex
and into the freedom of the Delhi night.

It's time, I say.
Annika pours petrol around the house,
up the walls, doors and shutters.
I hold the match, a flicker of destiny in my hand.

What are you waiting for?
Do it now, quickly!
Annika's body pulses with panic
but I have no such fear.

I allow the flame to kiss my fingertips,
before releasing it.
Rama moans,
we step away.

The flames waltz across the ground
drunkenly drinking up the petrol
dancing around our feet
thirsty to consume everything in their path.

The smell of burning petrol
takes hold of our senses,
smoke fills our lungs
as fire devours the walls of the building.

I can't help but smile,
seeing how the flames destroy everything so easily.
It pleases me to see it.
There's liberation in this destruction.

There's plenty more to turn to ash, Annika,
and self-made gods to topple from their self-made thrones
and from the parched earth something better will rise,
something new and fair, somewhere everyone can thrive.
This is our quest.
This is how we rise.
This is how we roar.

This is how we roar . . .
As Annika repeats our manifesto
I sense the words sticking in her throat.
We need to go, Rizu, before anyone sees us.

I'm transfixed by the flames,
feasting on the fiery image.
The cries, the chaos, the collapse –
it fills me up, feeds my spirit,
a wild dance of fury and pain.

Rama nudges as sirens wail in the distance.
It's time, I say.

And away we run.
From flames, from destruction,
the heat, the noise, the mess of it all.
I feel wild, free, untamed by fear.

They made me what I am,
I scream to the moon.
Spirit soaring,
running and leaping,
tripping and tearing
away from the heat of the flames
and into the heat of the night.

TWO

Beginnings

Let's rewind now.
Take it back to the beginning.
To the sparkly lights of India's capital city
where the upper-caste upper class
live comfortably behind large iron gates
protected and protecting their private colonies.

The wealthy thrive here,
they believe it's the only reason they are alive here
sitting on their marble verandas
believing they are safe here
better than everyone else here.
They feel invincible
masking their darkness behind shiny smiles.

Let's focus in on a white stone mansion,
one of eight in this gated illusion.
This one is home to the Malhotra family
a family whose life will change forever over the next few weeks
and in a room above a grand stairway is our Rizu,

as her old self
her ordinary self
not yet acquainted with her warrior self,
her hero self – Rizu.

Dreaming

I'm standing at the water's edge.
I dip my toe.
It's cold.
It's thrilling.

I feel my heart beat faster.
I want to wade in.
I'm scared.
I step back.

Stay, she says.

A woman.
I hadn't noticed her before,
standing beside me.

She looks like me.
An older me.
It is not me.

Don't run away, she says.

I want to say,
I'm not running away.
I do not.
My mouth won't open.
I'm frightened.
But only a little.

Don't be scared, she says.

Can she read my mind?
She holds out her hand.
I look at it.
I don't move my hand.
I just stare at her hand.
I look up.
I stare at her face.

She looks like me.
An older me.
It is not me.

I wake.

Something in the shadows

The dreams started small.
Abstract images, distant voices,
nothing was clear.
Like a whisper on the wind,
smoke from fire,
steam of a boiling kettle,
there, and then   gone.

Not enough to hold on to or understand,
just a sense of something and someone
out there trying to make contact.

At first I thought nothing of it –
just dreams, must be something I ate
or watched, or read, not real,
my subconscious processing the day,
my thoughts, my feelings.

But then they kept coming
night after night,
each one becoming clearer.
In the smoke now a shape
in the steam a scene
a voice on the wind.

Slowly forming into a woman
with a past that is mine,
a scene from another time
but one that's familiar
past and present colliding.

And now, she calls to me.
I am no longer a fly on the wall,
a silent watcher,
she is pulling me in,
she wants me to listen,
I am part of you, she says
not with words
but with her eyes
and then like smoke
she is   gone.

Infatuation

Butterflies dance in my stomach.

                                            `Sunny: Miss you.`

`Rizu: Miss you more.`

                                            `Sunny:` ♥

My heart pirouettes.

`Rizu: When can we be alone together?`

                                            `Sunny: Soon.`

I think about my next message carefully.
Mustn't annoy him.
Mustn't rush him.
Mustn't make him run away.
But
I need to know.
I need answers.
I need an end
to the secrets and lies.

`Rizu:   When are you going to tell her?`
`        I can't do this much longer. It's not fair.`
`        To her or me.`

Three dots ...
teasing
testing
taunting.

                    Sunny: Soon. Be patient.

I type fast.
My breath, shallow,
my face, hot.

Rizu: You've been saying this for the past two months.

                    Sunny: After her birthday.

So,
one more day?
Or one more week?
Or one more month?

Rizu: Promise?

                    Sunny: Promise.

He's promised before.
After the summer
after exams
after this, after that
always after something.

                    Sunny: Seriously though . . . 'Why me?' 😉

And just like that
despite knowing what's true
deep down
in my gut
I choose to believe it's different this time.
This time he means it.

I type quickly.

Rizu: 'Because you saw me when I was invisible.'

A quote from our favourite romcom,
a memory of the summer,
when it was just the two of us,
every day,
in our bubble.

> **Sunny: See you at school beautiful.** 😘

Rizu: 🖤🖤🖤

I lie back on my bed
phone on my chest
while butterflies dance in my stomach
and my heart pirouettes.

Mirror, mirror

Every morning the same dance.
To the left to the right, to the front to the back.
Suck it in, push them up, make that short, wear that long.
I twist, I turn, adjust and alter, contort and conform.

My body is a twisted joke,
too thin there, too thick here,
not the perfect in-between.
Clothes hang or cling, never quite right.

I turn away, hating the face, the body,
that stares back. Each flaw magnified,
eyes, too tired, smile, too forced,
each imperfection glaring,
the mirror's cruel honesty haunting.

Masking it

Hi guys! Your favourite girl Chandni here. Thanks for
joining me for today's tutorial –
tricks for higher cheekbones, tips for a thinner nose,
and that all-important lighter skin.
And don't start coming at me with your colourism BS
in the comments –
we all know lighter is brighter and brighter is better!

Let's get started . . .

I lean into the mirror.
I am dark, mud-like, dirt-like, monster-like.

I need those higher cheekbones
I need that thinner nose
I need that all-important lighter skin,
my creams, serums, foundations all laid out.

I apply one after the other just as instructed.
Emphasize cheekbones, highlight eyes, glossy lips, contoured nose.
The skin-lightening cream tingles, irritating my skin.
Breathe. 'Lighter is brighter – brighter is better.'

Now for my hair.
My hair.
My hair.
My hair.

Never perfect. A chaotic mess, frizzy, flat, a tangled disaster.
Flawless ads with flawless influencers,
perfect waves, cute and curly or sleek and straight,
mine a rebellion in every strand.

Layer after layer of concealers and foundation.
Lines to trick, colours to hide, gloss to disguise.
Pouting, pinching, blending to perfection
for a no-make-up unnaturally natural look.

But . . .

The contouring is not the same as it is on the video,
the lines aren't invisible, blending not working,
my skin looks cakey, not light, not bright
plastered in powder and foundation.

Wipe off and reapply
wipe off and reapply
wipe off and reapply.

I claw at my face,
I grab at my skin,
I look at my stomach
holding every inch of it in.

I feel exhausted, drained of light
keeping up with friends who shine so bright.
My every flaw behind a mask
holding me together piece by piece
all the parts that no one can see
inside this house, inside of me.

OK guys, that's all from me, your favourite girl Chandni.
Check back tomorrow for more tips and tricks.
Today's video was sponsored by Lighter Brighter Skincare.
Be sure to like and subscribe if you want to upgrade your look!

I'm sculpted, shaped, polished and painted.
Cheekbones defined, eyes concealing secrets,
lips glossed with lies, skin shaped by shadows and light.

I'm ready.

Eggshells

I hesitate for a moment outside my parents' bedroom
before knocking and slowly pushing the door ajar,
careful not to make a noise. I spy on my mother as she sleeps,
buried deep under the covers, rising and falling with her breath.

Don't just hover in the doorway, Rizu, are you in or out?
My father doesn't look up from his phone
scrolling through the news while stroking my mother's hair.
Sorry, Papa. I close the door behind me and kneel on the floor next to her.

Ma, I whisper, *I had that dream again.*
I wish you could tell me what it means, like you used to.
She reaches out her hand and without opening her eyes finds mine,
she holds it for a second, before sliding hers away
under the comfort of covers.

The painting towering over my parents' bed
tells the epic tale from the Mahabharata.
I loved listening to my mother tell the story
behind this painting when I was little.
The tale of Draupadi. Fierce feminine Draupadi.
How her fury and fire make her the true heroine of the Mahabharata.

I often wonder how my mother can sleep beneath this painting
and not rise every morning with a passion to seize the day.

There's a woman in the dream now,
before it was just a voice
but now I see a woman, it's so clear
she keeps calling –

Don't bother your mother, he says, cutting me off
before I can say, *to me . . . she keeps calling to me.*
I want to say, *it's unnerving and frightening*, but
most of all I want her to help me

                              talk to me

                                    hold me

like she used to.

Tolerated

Is there something else you want, Rizu?

It's Sonu's party tonight, I say.
I'll be getting ready at hers and staying the night.
He's yet to look at me.

OK. OK. That's all fine,
he says, waving his hand,
shooing me out the door.

Ma? She doesn't answer, she doesn't move,
only the contours of her body visible under the duvet.

She's resting, Rizu, he says.

She's not. I know she's not.
She doesn't want to engage,
preferring the comfort of her sheets
and the four walls of her room
to the outside world.

These days, like most days, my mother lies,
eyes closed, not sleeping. I can tell.
It's easier for her to pretend.
She has chosen to shut everything out.
Including me.

My father stays with her – as much as work allows.
Any spare moments outside the office are kept just for her.
I rarely see either of them.
He thinks it might make a difference to her mood.

It doesn't.
The only outcome –
I've lost them both.

My father lives for her,
all his time for her,
all the best therapy for her
and where does that leave me?
Alone.
With only the housekeeper for company.

Ma, I say again.

Shh, leave her be, he says. *Can't you see she's resting?*

How much rest does she need?

Finally, he looks up,
a thunderstorm across his face.

I slowly make my way out of their room.
He strokes her hair,
I hover in the doorway,
jealous of their love
and wonder why
there's not enough
to share with me.

Genetics

I worry my mother's melancholy
will bleed into me,
it'll seep in and settle under my skin.

If I'm honest, I think it already has.
I can feel it sometimes.

A pressure, pulling and pushing
and I'm drowning, desperate
to catch a breath but
I'm slowly being swallowed whole.

Some days are darker,
draped in a fog so dense it smothers
and it is slow, and it groans.

Nobody ever tells you that.
The sound steals something from you,
fills the emptiness with a nameless weight.

I see why she sleeps.
There's no space for anything else.

It makes a stranger of you.
My own reflection, unrecognizable
like I'm wearing someone else's skin.

It sends me spiralling, wanting to
scrape it all off and start again
as someone new, somewhere else
away from the strain of sadness.

I can't help but wonder . . .
is it just hers?
Or is it mine now too?

Awake

The latest Bollywood tune
plays out on the radio
and the reporter gives a rundown
of the latest news,
each story worse than the one before.

Three sisters ...
Burned to death in a village in Uttar Pradesh ...
The rise in witch-hunting continuing to grow ...
The radio cracks –
The vigilante group led by Shalini Devi
condemns these attacks ...

Another cheery track distracts me from reality
and as I close my parents' bedroom door
I catch a glimpse of my mother's eyes opening.

Meena

Ill at ease

I open my eyes
just as Rizu pulls the door closed behind her.

Shalini . . .
Her name sends ripples of unease
through my body.
I should be used to it by now.
I am not.

Each time I hear it
a wave of needles
cascades through me,
leaving a million tiny tears.

Backward village people, Raaj tuts.

Like me? I say.

You were never like the others.

I move my body away from his.

Don't, he says. *Sorry. I love you.*

I can't say it back.
I try to.
But I've been numb for so long
it seems impossible to feel anything.

It's OK, he says.
*You don't have to say it back.
I can love enough for the both of us.*

Almost real

The morning is heavy and humid. I sit at the table,
a golden gleam from the chandelier cuts through the room
casting dancing diamonds of light around us.
I watch Jaya fold napkins, small and precise, like her.

Sit with me, have some breakfast, I say.

I have so much to do, she says.

Just ten minutes, pleeeeeease.
I stick out my bottom lip.

Fine, she says. *For you, anything.*

Jaya and I – we eat breakfast together sometimes.
Something you shouldn't do.
'Never eat with the help,' they say.
Those people who wear caste like a badge,
who wouldn't dream of letting someone like Jaya touch their china.
My mother has always said,
You only need to walk around the city, Rizu,
ignorance knows no borders, no class, no caste, it's everywhere.
Treat people fairly, always.

Jaya smiles a quiet smile and sits across from me.
I ask about her family, her home, and her stories spill out.
She shows me a video of her younger sister
chasing kites along rooftops.

And that, Jaya says, eyes narrowing,
is how she broke her arm.
Honestly, there is no taming that girl.

I smile. I nod. I chew.
Sometimes I think Jaya's the only real thing in this big house
where gleaming chandeliers distract from the truth.
Like tea into toast, I soak in her stories,
not because I'm hungry, but because I'm lonely.

She laughs and I laugh as I talk about school
and she talks about her life before she came to live with us,
and we share this strange, soft thing, this friendship –
if that's what it is, if that's what it can be,
and I wonder, is Jaya kind because she must be?

I tell her about exams, the boys,
she talks about her uncle still in the village,
still waiting for rain that doesn't come.
And here we are, in this house, this house that isn't a home,
eating breakfast like we belong, even though
I know she'll never sit here when others are watching
and she knows that I'd never ask.

I hope Jaya knows how much I cling to these moments,
our quiet communion across caste.
How much I need this, need her,
more than the silver spoons and marble floors.
More than the title tucked behind my name.

Jaya, my almost-sister, my almost-friend.
Maybe it's all an illusion, an arrangement
but still, I'll take it.
I'll take the crumbs of connection
and pretend they fill me up.

Best friends

I sit in the car,
grateful for the A/C blasting through.
The morning is muggy,
the weight of it sticky and stifling.
Santosh, our family driver, turns on the ignition.

Santosh, Sonu is riding with us today.

Of course, maam, he says, pulling on the handbrake.

A knock on the car window
and there she is,
the most popular girl in school.
All glossy and slim, big eyes, wide smile.
She opens the door, slides in next to me,
smooth as silk.

So, you gonna wish me happy birthday or what?

Indian gold

Happy Birthday, Sonu.
Birthday present now or later? I ask,
teasing the gift bag in front of her.

Now, bitch!
She snatches the present out of my hand
and tears it open.
I watch her closely as she
rips off the paper, screeching, *Gold!*
before opening the box.

I watch as she puts the bracelet on her wrist.
You like it? I ask
my voice caught in my throat
like jewellery pulled too tight
like the smile I'm faking.
I love it! she says,
and I'm bursting to tell her my secret
wrapped up in guilt
and suddenly I'm wrapped up in hugs
and squeals and smiles and laughter.

There's something special about Indian gold.
It shines different.
Not like cheap glitter that fades with time,
but with a weight, a warmth,
it's heavy with history
and when you give it, you feel it,
you feel the weight of everything it holds.

I wonder, as the gold catches her eye,
does it shimmer bright enough to hide my secret?
Does it reflect enough light to drown out what haunts me?
Does Indian gold shine strong enough to mask the betrayal I wear?

Seventeen

It's been in the planning
since sweet sixteen.
Now, sweet sixteen was *fine*
but sweet seventeen will be better,
sweet seventeen will be bigger.

Sweet seventeen's not just a party,
it's the event of the year.
There'll be celebrities, photographers,
live music and more.
Only Delhi's most desirable
will attend this ball.

Sweet sixteen was fine but
sweet seventeen will be *legendary*.

Sonu will shine, dripping in jewels,
her seat at the top secured,
her status as queen bee etched in the stars.
India's most eligible –
her ranking decided, her reign recognized.

Sweet sixteen was fine
but sweet seventeen will *soar*.

Sitting high on her throne
rich and ready to be seen.
People will talk long after the night fades
and the city will hum with her name.

Sweet sixteen was fine but
sweet seventeen will be better.
Much better.

The first call

Delhi traffic, wild and weaving as always.
A chaos of tuk-tuks and motorbikes crawling forward.
Homework waits beneath the honking of horns.
I pull out *The Crucible*
and begin speed-reading,
racing to the part I should have reached.

Oh my God, I can't believe you're actually reading that.
Sonu swoops in, snatching the book from my hand.
Just watch the film. It's easier.

I like reading it, I say, taking it back.
Films always skip things.

It's my birthday! she cries.
Her eyes wide and pleading,
her voice dripping with drama.
I want your full attention.
Pleeeeeease.

Fine, I say, closing the book.
How was your morning?

Oh, you know.
Usual fanfare.
Presents, balloons,
so over the top.

She looks down as she speaks
and in the pause, I notice
the skin under her eyes –
slightly swollen.

Everything OK? I ask.

Yah of course, why wouldn't it be.
She smiles,
gloss and sparkle returning to her face,
like the sun forcing its way through clouds.

The radio hums
repeating stories of witch hunts,
Shalini Devi and her fearless, fierce female army.
The voice speaks of Shalini's courage
her bravery, her activism, her prowess
and *that* tiger –
the terror that stalks beside her
chasing fear into everyone she confronts.

Vigilante more like.
Sonu looks at me,
Don't you think?

I don't know,
one person's vigilante is another person's hero.

My mum says she's a witch,
and her so-called army . . .
More like a cult –
a coven of sorts.

Witches aren't real, Sonu.

Sonu shrugs,
her interest drifting.
This is boring, Santosh. Play some music!

As Santosh changes the station
the sound skips,
Shalini's voice drops in and out
and then, in the static
a voice breaks through.
I hear it, clear as day –
Rizu, it says, *Rizu.*

Mind games

Am I losing my mind?
Is it slipping through the seams?

At what point does hearing your name in the empty air
mean you've crossed a line?
The line between sane and something else,
something wild, something untamed,
something creeping at the edges.

Am I losing my mind?
Or is it real?
Is someone out there pulling me in?
Whispering in the wind,
shifting in the shadows.

Not mine

The sun is hitting just right
so we pull down our shades,
arm in arm shining bright,
strutting into our favourite cafe with flair
like we own it, without a care.

We claim our corner, iced coffees in hand
scrolling through socials, waiting for the gang.
I sneak a snap with my icy delight,
post it on socials – Sunny's first to hit *like*!
I smile at the screen, feeling the spike.

Then, in he comes, playing it cool,
sneaking up behind her, a finger to his lips,
as I stand, heart sinking, looking like a fool.
His arms wrap round her, holding her tight,
making Sonu squeal with pure delight.
Happy birthday, baby, he says smooth as a song
then winks at me like I'm to play along.

I noticed him first, it's true.
There was something about the way he stood,
he made the air swell, it sparked something new.
I watched as he laughed, his smile electric,
moments passed and I wished he would turn,
to catch my eye, a smile, a glance,
to give me hope, give me a chance.

But then Sonu walked in, and everything changed.
In a heartbeat, my world felt rearranged.
I had to watch it unfold, feeling the sting,
ignoring the ache his presence would bring.

Until now,
until this summer.
Just one more day, I tell myself again,
then the truth will be out,
but until then I'll remind my heart,
he is hers and we're worlds apart.

Popular girls

The gang is here,
Preeti, Mia, Tanya and me.
Each of us in our rightful place
behind our queen, Sonu,
the one who runs the hive.

We hike up our skirts,
shades low, arm in arm,
side by side, in perfect sync.
We are the popular girls, turning heads,
hair falling like waves,
gliding through the school gates.

Preeti's smile lights up like a flame,
Mia's laughter like a burst of fireflies,
Tanya sparkles like a firework,
and Sonu – Sonu ignites the air around her.

I watch how others are drawn to her, pulled in,
like gravity got stronger when she walked into the school.

I wonder how they all make it look so easy.
My hair falls like theirs,
like waves, it shines and shimmers,
yet why am I on the sidelines,
stuck on the shore,
watching everyone drift towards them?

How do they do it?
Is it something learned,
or is it stitched into their skin?

Is it in the tilt of their head,
or the curve of their voice?
Or something more,
something deeper,
something I'll never touch.

No matter how my hair falls,
it's a magic I can't quite hold.

Gossip

In the toilets we apply more lipstick
and engage in gossip.
Faking injury to miss PE
just so we can talk reality TV.
Passing notes in class
to help time pass
our chatter flows back and forth between
Indian Matchmaker and *The Real Housewives of Mumbai*,
and opinions on the new girl in school
who just transferred from Seoul.

Apparently, she knows a K-pop group
she's like related to a member or something, says Sonu.

And then we deliberate
on whether that's true
or if she's a liar.
We conclude the latter.

She didn't seem friendly,
like a bit of a bitch.

Her eyeliner doesn't help,
makes her look like a witch!

And a cackle erupts between us
as we stalk the halls
hunting our next victim.

Crucible

Our set text for this term is *The Crucible* by Arthur Miller.

I love Abigail, says Sonu. *She's my favourite.*

New girl shakes her head.
But she's ruthless – so many innocent lives lost because of her.

Maybe. Sonu shrugs, unbothered.
But she was betrayed, shamed by Proctor.
He deserved everything he got.
If I were her, I'd do the same.

Sonu's words hang heavy in the air,
like a storm cloud ready to break,
a truth she's waiting to play out.

Interesting, says Madame Anand,
trying not to look troubled by Sonu's statement.
But why did Miller write it?

A metaphor for McCarthyism, I say.
He wanted to show how brutal persecution
can rise again, any time, any place.
How hysteria can spread based on suspicion and fear
rather than evidence.

Very good, Miss Malhotra. Can anyone tell me
what fuels the hysteria in The Crucible?

Sonu's hand is up. *Religion, Madame Anand.*
And, in Abigail's case, personal vendettas.

Very good, Miss Jain.
Yes, Abigail's actions result in tragic consequences.

Her accusations of witchcraft, I say,
set off a chain of events that allow that hysteria to flourish.

How so, Miss Malhotra?

People feared being seen as an outsider.
If you're an outsider, you might be accused,
so better to join in, be part of the pack,
even if you don't believe what's being said.
It's still going on, Madame Anand,
all over the world in different ways.

Elaborate, Miss Malhotra.

Well, on the news they are saying witch-hunting is on the rise across India.
Hysteria is spreading through communities.
It's happening right here, Madame. It's scary.

Madame Anand smiles.
No need to worry, Miss Malhotra,
those crimes stem from ignorance, a lack of education.
I doubt they will travel any further than the villages.

Rizu found her way out of the village, says Vikesh,
his words like a dart, aimed right at me.
I turn, throat bound, eyes burning.

Before I have a chance
to think of a witty comeback
Sonu has my back.

Rizu was born in Delhi, stupid, and just because
her mother wasn't born into money, she's still a Brahmin,
and she's a teacher and very well educated.
Check your facts.
Sonu winks at me and mouths,
You OK?

I nod. Guilt and shame
soaking into my skin.

Well, Madame Anand, my mother once told me,
you only need to walk around the city,
ignorance knows no borders, no class, no caste, it's everywhere.
Like in this classroom . . .

I stare at Vikesh.
I want the words to strike a chord
but his laughter cuts through.
Learn how to take a joke, jeez, he says.

Fine, Madame Anand interrupts,
let's talk about this rise in witch hunts.
Firstly, does anyone know the earliest recordings of witch trials in India?
Silence.
Seventeen ninety-two. The Santhal Witch Trials in Jharkhand.
Many were murdered in the most barbaric way . . .

Evocation

A shiver slides down my spine.
My body starts to ache
and my jaw throbs.
I steady myself,
palms pressed on the desk,
trying not to fall apart.

The smell of smoke.
I'm choking.
My lungs burning.
My breath blocked.
I gasp for air.

Can't breathe.
Can't breathe,
I whisper.

And then – darkness.
I'm down,
I'm drowning,
flames all around me.

Rizu? What's wrong with you? Rizu, speak to me.

Madame Anand shakes my shoulders,
her voice pulling me back,
the pain, the burning, it fades
just like that.

Classmates looking at me,
mouths open in shock,
or staring and sniggering.

I'm here
on the floor,
no flames, no smoke,
just exposed and shaken.

Miss Jain, Madame Anand says, looking at Sonu,
her face a map of worry,
take Miss Malhotra to the nurse.

Deflect

The nurse's room is clinical and cold.
Sonu puts her arm round me,
What was that all about?

I don't know, I say
wondering how I could even begin
to describe what happened.

*It's my birthday, couldn't you wait
to have a nervous breakdown next week?*

I can't speak.
I'm too shook-up,
too freaked out by
the visions,
the voices,
the dreams,
and now this . . .

*Hey, maybe it's the school ghost, Gia,
trying to possess you so she can have her revenge!*
She waves her fingers in front of me
and puts on a spooky voice.
It's irritating but I laugh.
At least I made you smile, she says.

The nurse pokes and prods.
I open my mouth and *Ahhh*,
she takes my pulse,
checks my blood pressure,
asks if I've eaten
and drunk enough water.
Yes and *Yes*.

She concludes it was a panic attack
brought on by stress.
I nod and agree and tell her I'll rest.

As we walk out the room
Sonu grabs my arm.
No rest tonight though.
It's my birthday.

I know, I know, I'll still be there don't worry.

And then she hits me with it.

Do you think Sunny is being weird?

The muscles in my face tense.
How do you mean?

I don't know. I think he might be seeing someone else.
He sent me a text this morning.
I don't think it was meant for me.
Well, I know it wasn't.
I was going to reply
but then he deleted it
and . . . I don't know . . .

There's a tremor in her voice,
she bites her bottom lip.

What did it say? I ask.

It was weird, it just said,
'Seriously though why me?'
and then a winky kissing face emoji.

I feel the blood drain from my face.
I wouldn't read into that, I say quickly.
I don't think that means anything.
My heart races.
I look for clues.
Does she know?
Is this a test?
Don't be silly, I continue,
he would never.

True, she says after a moment.
Why would he trade gold for a tin can.
I feel her studying me.
I swallow panic.

You really don't look well, she says.
Maybe we should go back to the nurse.

Stolen moments

He is not mine,
but somehow, we steal moments.
A fleeting look in the hall,
a smile in the cafeteria,
a brush of fingertips in class,
a hand pressed softly against my waist at the school gates.

He is not mine,
and still, we find ways –
a secret text,
a coded word,
our arms grazing as if by chance,
close enough to feel his breath against my skin.

He is not mine,
but these moments keep building,
this crush, this craving,
it's too real to ignore.

He is not mine,
yet
I tell myself it's love, it must be love,
I would never do this if it weren't for love.
I would never live for these stolen moments
for less than love.

Delhi night

We step into Delhi's night,
where the air is heavy with heat.
Cars honk, a city that never sleeps.

We're dressed in our sequined gowns and high heels
clicking against a cracked pavement, a little unsteady.

It's sweet seventeen,
everything organized and going to plan.
Photographers and celebs,
we pose with poise.

I see Sunny in the haze,
Sonu wraps her arms round him.
I tug at my dress, hips swaying
and for a moment we share a look,
Sunny and I,
it's quick and quiet
but I feel it.

We are here to party,
feeling like stars in the chaos.
We push through the club door,
bass thumping, heartbeat heavy.
It's packed, bodies pressed against bodies,
moving together in the dim-lit room,
sweat rolling down spines,
the air buzzing with heat.

Inside this place I feel wild.
The music vibrates through my entire body,
dancing shoulder to shoulder,
the drinks flow
and lines blur.

Sunny pulls me aside –
into a dark corner,
hidden from the crowd.

Somebody will see, Sunny.

Don't worry, she's posing for photographs.

My eyes dart around the club. *It's not safe.*

You worry too much.

He slips his arms round me.
The music plays, louder and faster,
the DJ's got everyone jumping
and belting out lyrics,
but in this moment, it's just us,
between the smoke, the sweat,
and the noise of Delhi's never-ending night.

Summer nights

This summer, I was his and he was mine.
And Sonu? Out of sight, out of mind.

That first kiss caught us both off guard.
I told myself it was nothing,
we forgot who we were meant to be,
caught up in a moment, wild and free.

But then, we lingered, and it felt so right.
It's easy with you, Sonu always picks fights.
Believing him, I leaned in closer, I couldn't resist,
his kiss was gentle, a rush I couldn't quit.

I didn't mean to betray her, so I whispered her name.
She's in London, chasing English boys,
Sunny would say. Convincing himself, convincing me too,
that what we were sharing was honest and true.

But some nights, when the world was quiet,
guilt curled around me like a ghost.
I loved her like a sister, but love made me blind,
made me selfish, reckless, unkind.

And as the weeks drifted by,
I chose to forget,
falling deep
no signs of regret.

What I had with Sunny felt real and profound.
I convinced myself of every sweet lie
and for those five weeks of summer,
we soared so high, like nothing could break us, not even the sky.

The two of us were lost in each other's embrace
until Sonu returned and so did Sunny, straight into her arms,
leaving me adrift and unseen
feeling the sharp sting of love's cruel charms.

Caught

We inch closer
the space between us vanishing
forgetting where we are
forgetting who we are
wanting to disappear into the darkness.

He pulls me in
his breath entwined with mine
his fingers in my hair
my hand round his neck.

I'm weightless, floating,
these few stolen minutes
stretching into hours.
Time bends, the air vibrates.

I'm no longer myself
with Sunny the mask falls off.
I don't know the girl underneath
she's never been allowed to speak.

But then, we break for air
and there she is.

Her face twisted with fury.

You. She spits the word
her eyes locked on mine.
You.

Sonu

Hurt

Standing, staring
still as a stone.

I keep my rage inside.
I hold back.
I walk away.
I don't say a word.
Numb.
My mind a mess,
swamped by a million thoughts,
a noise I can't mute.

How could they do this?
Why would my friend betray me like that?
When did it start?
Was this the first time?
How long has it been going on?

Rage rises, rumbling beneath my ribs.
By the time I reach home
I'm boiling, burning,
hot tears flowing,
humiliation seared into my skin.

I'll never forgive them.
Not her.
Not him.
But especially not Rizu.

When a friend betrays you,
it's a different sort of pain.
A lover lies – that's almost expected.
Desire can be shallow,
fading with time.

But a friend's deceit –
that cuts deeper.
She knew my heart,
my fears,
and yet she still smiled in my face.
I trusted her,
I bared my soul to her,
she saw the cracks
and filled them with lies.

For him to break my heart,
it's expected.
But her?
Pretending,
smiling,
humiliating me.
The one I thought would always have my back.
She'll pay,
I'll make sure of that.

She'll know what it feels like
to lose something
you never thought could be taken.
Because in the end,
it wasn't him I trusted the most,
it was *her*.

One way or another
I will ruin Rizu.

Fate

So this is the moment
that sees everything change.
Fingers will point,
an innocent will take the blame.

In this unfolding story
no one is spared
and no one is safe.
Fate has sealed each final place.

Rizu and Sonu
their end is set.
Both will die,
no more bets.

THREE

Hallucinations

I spend the entire weekend
holed up in my bedroom.
I have a choice: to fight, take flight or freeze.

I am frozen.

In a trance of sorts.
The ground beneath me shifts and shakes.
A tidal wave of guilt, greed, desire, dread
all come crashing in.
Days turn to night in a blur of tears,
as the hours creep closer to Monday.

The night before school I get zero sleep.
I toss and turn.
I retch and wail in the bathroom
but nothing comes up.
I want this feeling to leave my body
I want to disappear, to dissolve –
my life is ruined,
Sonu forgives no one.

As I lie in a sleepless sleep
the woman from my dreams
comes to me again
floating into my room
like we share the same space.

I am paralysed by fear.
Flesh faltering, refusing to move.
I stare, caught in her gaze
as she holds out her haunting arms.

Follow me, she whispers.
I try to answer
but my mouth is zipped up.

She glides closer
moving towards me
until she hovers right above, smiling.

Don't be frightened, she says.
Be brave.
You're not alone.

She reaches forward
arms outstretched
like she wants to embrace.
She floats closer and closer
until she disappears into me and I wake
screaming into the suffocating darkness.

Blocked

I spend the early hours of Monday morning,
fingers restless sending messages to Sunny
still panicked, desperate to undo our betrayal,
erase the summer, wipe it clean.
I regret it all.

Despite Sunny not answering my messages all weekend
I persist.

Rizu: Are you going into school today?

Three dots appear
                      and
                                      disappear.

Rizu: Have you messaged Sonu? Have you heard from her?

Three dots appear
                      and
                                      disappear.

I stare at the phone,
the silence stretches on,
seconds feeling like hours,
my thoughts race, my body restless.

Rizu: Hello?
Sunny?
Why are you ignoring me???????

My heart thrums a frantic beat
waiting for a text that never comes.

Rizu: Sunny! Answer me!

This time it doesn't send.
I try again – message not sent.
I try another ten times – message not sent.
I scream, throwing my phone across the room.
It crashes against the dresser,
knocking over make-up,
sending a photo of Sonu and me laughing on holiday
smashing to the floor.

Everything OK, maam?
Jaya's small voice slips under the door.

Yes, I snap.

Sorry, maam.

No, I'm sorry.
My breath caught between
each word as tears escape down my face
and Jaya opens the door.

I'm sorry, I choke on the words,
the crying uncontrollable now.

It's OK. Shh.
She strokes my hair,
Tell me, tell me everything.

But I can barely speak.
I'm too tangled in Sonu
too swallowed by Sunny
too drowning in my own self-loathing.

Jaya listens to it all without judgement.
I have been cruel, pushing her away all weekend,
now here she is, cloaking me in her warmth,
whispering soft words of comfort,
soothing my tears,
holding my hand through the ache of it all,
and telling me,
You're not alone in this darkness, I promise.

I feel alone, I confess.
*I can't go into school
it'll be torture,
god only knows what Sonu will do.
Everyone will stare, everyone will talk.*

*This thing will blow over, trust me.
Love makes us all crazy,
you'll be friends by the end of the day.
Come, you'll feel better after some breakfast.*

I'm not hungry.

*None of that. The only way to mend a troubled heart
is through food. I'll make your favourite.*
She gives me a hug, a cocoon of comfort
that quiets my fears.

With Jaya I'm always reminded
that even in chaos, I'm always held.

Take courage

I catch my reflection in the mirror
eyes swollen, face blotched.
I'm hideous.
I can't face school.
I can't face Sonu.
Not like this.

Then, I see her again . . .
just for a second
looking back at me from the glass
and she whispers.

But to hide will be worse.
It will prolong the pain.

I close my eyes.
Open them.
She's still there.
A woman.
In the mirror.
Smiling.

I consider calling Jaya,
see if she sees what I see.
No.
The fewer people know about these visions,
the better.
For now,
I'll keep them to myself.

Your fate is sealed.
Walk through the fire now

and control the flames
or hide and forever be its victim.

Shut up! I scream to an empty room.
I take a deep breath
and close my eyes again.
I want the vision to go away.

When I open them
I'm relieved to see she is gone.
I sigh with relief. *Good.*

I look beyond my reflection
taking a moment to think about what could be.
Maybe it *is* best to face Sonu.
To talk to her,
tell her it was nothing
that she means more to me
than a boy ever could.

I'll tell her I was drunk.
I couldn't stand up straight
let alone think straight.
I was totally out of it,
surely she could tell.

Yes, this sounds right,
this, Sonu might believe.
I'm convinced it's true
and ready my mask for the day.

Sonu will forgive me
and all will be well
by the end of play.

Ignored

I spot him at the school gates.
He swaggers in, I swiftly take my chance,
standing in front of him, the silence between us
thick like fog.

I take a breath, step forward,
hoping for a smile, a spark of recognition,
but he looks down,
like a cloud passing over the sun,
the warmth between us, now cold.

Hey, my voice weak,
he turns away and moves on,
and I am left, standing, alone,
feeling the weight of those unanswered texts
and the memories of what once was.

Accused

We meet in the bustling hall.
Sonu seems slow and sure,
protected from the students' gaze
by oversized tinted glasses.
Preeti, Mia and Tanya,
a human shield,
stand beside her.
How could you?
they chant in unison
walking past me.

Everyone has heard.
Everyone knows.
News spreads fast in this school.
Everyone was at the party
everyone saw
everyone talks.

The party.
The betrayal.
The drama.

They're all desperate to see
the one who's broken,
the boy who betrayed,
and the girl who came between them.

The victim.
The cheat.
The slut.

I stand alone,
Sonu stands with her army,
unmoving, unreadable,
behind those dark glasses.

Can we talk? I ask
my voice barely holding.

There's literally nothing you could say to me.
Her voice cold and unforgiving.

Please, Sonu, just let me explain.

I thought we were friends. Best friends.

I reach out my hand, desperate.
I'm sorry,
I say, grabbing her wrist,
stopping her from walking away.

Let go of me, she hisses.
She struggles to pull away but I hold on.

Please, I'm begging you, Sonu.
My heart thrumming, fingers quivering.

I said, let go!
She wrenches herself free,
venom in her voice.
*Get away from me,
you evil witch!*

Witch

Ah! It burns! It burns!
she cries, clutching her wrist
like it's on fire.

I laugh, confused.
I look around at the crowd
that's now closing in.

What are you talking about? I ask.

Oh my God! You burned me!

Sonu?
Is this a joke?
I look to the crowd
phones raised, capturing the scene.
I barely touched her, I say.

You're trying to curse me! she shrieks,
as screens light up my face,
bursts of brightness piercing my eyes.

Curse you? Are you serious? Sonu?

Sonu turns to her gang.
Look, she burned me, she cries. *She burned me!*

Oh my God, they gasp
eyes wide with horror,
look what she did to you!

I can't see it.
I can't see what they see.
I look at my hands.
Is it possible I hurt her?
Did I scorch her skin?

Just stay away from me. Witch!
The word ripples through the hall.

The crowd comes in closer
phones shoved in my face.

Leave me alone! I scream.
My voice raw and breaking.
I feel weak, trapped,
cornered and caged.

Wild fire

By lunchtime, it's already spreading.
Sonu's sparked a supernatural story.
It feeds on whispers and burns its way down the halls.

Hundreds of phones flicker with the same flame,
a flicker that spreads to a hundred more.
Everyone's talking, all eyes on me.
I can feel the heat, like fire is already licking at my skin.

By the end of the day
they're all watching
videos and pictures,
me burning Sonu
with nothing but my touch,
blazing across the internet.

I'm stuck,
pinned under the glow of my phone
scrolling, scrolling, scrolling.
Jaya covers the screen with her hand.
Don't look any more.
I brush it away.
I need to know what they're saying.
She holds me,
seeing how I'm falling apart
and knowing she's the only one who can keep me together.
We watch the scene play on repeat.

Ah! It burns! It burns!
What are you talking about?
Oh my God! You burned me.
Sonu? I barely touched her.
You're trying to curse me!
Curse you? Are you serious? Sonu?
Look, she burned me. She burned me!
Oh my God, look what she did to you!
Just stay away from me. Witch!
Leave me alone!

The flames rise.
Three thousand. Four thousand.
Ten thousand. Twenty thousand.
Every share, every comment
another log on the fire.

Hundreds of comments.

Is this real?
        Yes it's real.
                I know her, her family does black magic.

I click on the profile,
a stranger's face stares back.
And then there's another
and another,
people claiming to know me
making up lies
all to keep the flames alive.

As I scroll and scroll

unable to switch off
one name keeps coming up,
a name from long ago,
a name that made our school famous
from a story half forgotten,
a twisted tale chopped and changed.
One name is resurfacing –

Gia.

Gia

They say it happened late one night
a group of friends
no ordinary girls
something darker –
a cult
witches casting spells
behind closed doors.

An initiation,
a ritual for power
but something went wrong.
The fire they summoned grew too hot
the air too thick with too much smoke.

A girl, Gia, too young
too eager to belong
died before she could scream.

It's a story kept alive
to frighten fresh meat.
Some say you can still hear her
if you're in the school after hours.
Gia, the girl who died,
her voice caught between the walls.
Others swear they've seen her in mirrors
her eyes wide, frozen in fear
as if the spell never let her go.

And the leader of the cult –
the one who started it all,
the one who dabbled in dark magic
for desire and the devil
was . . .

Meena Malhotra.
My mother.

They say I'm here
adding names to a list,
to finish what my mother started,
to carry out the devil's wish.

Denial

It's a lie,
it must be a lie.

Why haven't I heard this before?
Surely, she would have shared it,
I'd be the first to know, right?

It's a lie,
it must be a lie.

Just a rumour,
a twisted tale, spinning stories,
everyone's out to get me.

It's a lie,
it must be a lie.

Gia, her story has echoed through the halls,
a legend whispered in corners
and now it clings to me.

It's a lie,
it must be a lie.

Yet the truth gnaws at me.

Lost

My voice breaks as I roar.
The sound is small
still not yet fully formed.

Jaya flings her arms round me.
Shh. Shh. Try and stay calm.
It's a lie, it's all lies.

How can you be so sure?

Because I know your mother.
She looks at me. *Do you believe it?*

Answers

Jaya tries pulling me back,
she tries calming me down,
but I am a force she can't contain.

I grab my mother,
I pull her out of bed.
I need her to open her eyes.
I need her to see me standing here
falling apart.

I need her to tell me her name is not linked to this.
No way did she ever, would ever . . .
I need her to tell me it's a cruel joke.
Online trolls are adding fuel to the fire.

I need her to tell me none of this is true.

Meena

A secret

I watch the video.
I read the comments.

Secrets, things long buried
now clawing their way to the surface,
running wild
shaking the ground beneath our feet.

I know too well how whispers grow into storms,
how they unravel lives.
There are ghosts in my past,
truths I've kept buried

but now all that's hidden has been unearthed
and I have no choice
but to face what I did.

Twisted

A tale gets twisted over time.
Bits get added
and embellished,
it's all about selling a story.

Add a little bit of this,
and a little bit of that,
turn a story round
twist it into fact.

Every ear that hears
will add a little something more,
a cruel whisper
growing louder with every lie added.

This is how a tale is twisted
and monsters are made,
fiction turned to fact
embedded in fable.

Truth

It didn't unfold as they say,
no whispers of spells,
no circles drawn in shadows,
just a tale twisted by time.

I was one of three taken
late one night.
Gia, the scholarship girl
me, the village girl
and my friend, from money, just like them
but who dared to befriend
two girls who didn't quite fit.

No rituals, no magic,
just rich girls with too much power
and too little heart.

They laughed as they pushed us,
tumbling down to the basement,
beneath the kitchen's hum,
their 'fun' cloaked in malice,
a prank spun out of control,
and when it shattered,
Gia paid the price.

Tied and tested,
they fed on our fear,
no escape, no scream,
bound and gagged,
our voices silenced.

They loathed Gia,
they wanted her gone.
My friend and I – the do-gooders,
tainted by association,
we needed to be taught a lesson,
and Gia, forced from our school.

They despised us for welcoming her,
for threatening their order,
for making people from a different caste
feel equal.

When I close my eyes, I still see it.
I pause, trying to steady my breath.
Rizu grips my hand.
Please, Ma, don't stop. I need to know.

I inhale deeply.
They kicked, they punched,
burned us with cigarettes,
made us drink a putrid brew
that wrenched our insides.

But Gia –
she needed her medicine,
her illness overlooked
as they pushed and forced
causing pain for their own sick games.
And when she fell,
her life fading away,
they fled the scene,
money and power shielding them,
the school covered up where they'd been.

*We were silenced,
told to utter no word,
I kept the truth buried.
That's my sin.*

*So, you see,
there was no cult, no witches,
but something darker,
a game I never wished to play.*

*I look at my daughter,
her face etched with confusion.
If that's the truth, Ma,
then why do they say you led?
Why do they say you're the witch
who killed Gia?*

*I take her hands in mine.
It's no coincidence,
your falling-out with Sonu
has stirred the past.
There was one girl from that night,
now entwined in our lives,
a woman who revels in twisting tales
for her daughter's sake.*

Who, Ma?

Kareena Jain.

Sonu's ma?

A long silence settles,
before Rizu finds her words again.
Why didn't you tell me?
I would never have been her friend!

Oh Rizu, I can't choose your friends.
Kareena and I share a mutual dislike,
threatening each other's worlds,
but you and Sonu –
you found each other in preschool,
never letting go.
What could we do?
You would both scream to the heavens
if we tried to keep you apart.

Rizu's hands slip from mine,
her gaze searching my face.
Do you regret not speaking up, Ma?

Every day.
Not a day passes
without guilt or shame.
My voice wavers.
My best friend spoke up,
disgusted by my silence
she roared and called them out.
But no one listened.
These girls had power on their side,
and were therefore protected.

After that she left the school,
vanished from my life,
saying my silence mirrored their cruelty.
Maybe she's right.
I didn't speak when it mattered
and it's haunted me for years.

Who was this friend, Ma?
Rizu's eyes seek answers.
I have worn this silence
like a noose round my neck,
it's time to let go.

Shalini, I whisper.
My friend's name was Shalini.

Shalini

Shalini –
the woman with the tiger
the warrior
the legend
the activist
the leader
the saviour
the goddess
reborn in flesh –
***that** Shalini?*

Yes, she says
as cool as a sea breeze
like knowing one of the most
formidable women in the country
isn't a big deal.

Why have you never told me?

Because to tell you would
mean dragging out a past
I've fought to bury.

So, what is she like?

It's been almost thirty years –
her voice wrapped in memory
– how would I know what she's like now?

Ma, this is huge!
She has a tiger as a bodyguard.
What a badass.

She smiles.
Well, she always did like to make an impression.

What else do you remember about her?

She was a wild tempest
brave as lightning splitting the sky
fierce, like a mother wolf
and utterly unforgiving.

Answers

I have to ask.
Not to be cruel
but because the need to know
consumes me.

Is that why you locked yourself away?
Forgot me,
forgot yourself,
trapped in sleep?

Stop, she says,
her voice quakes.
I never forgot you.
I lost myself, yes –
but not you,
never you.
I've never not wanted
to be your mother.
The trauma of that night
the weight of it,
I can't bear it.
I still see her, you know,
I still see Gia,
every time I close my eyes.
But you,
you were always in my heart.
Sometimes life turns you inside out
and no matter how much you claw at the seams
you can't stitch yourself back together.

I worry, I say,
I worry I'm like you –
turned inside out,
broken.
I feel it
the darkness,
it lingers in me too,
like a scar beneath my skin.

I falter, my voice edged with fear.

What if I can't fix it?

Meena

Origins

Let me tell you a story, Rizu.
Before all of this
before the roar of your birth
before times started to repeat
before things left in the past
became the things of the present.
On the outskirts of Bundelkhand,
in the Badlands of India
where law and order
tread a thin line
is a place I used to call home . . .

Legend

On the banks of the River Chambal
a place of ravines and rocky mountains
where dacoits reign
and rain causes chaos,
drowning or droughts,
Draupadi's curse rules over its people,
she has taken over the game of dice now.

You see, there is a myth
surrounding my birthplace.
The legend of Charmanwati.

Legend has it that a game of dice
took place around Charmanwati –
the ancient name of the Chambal River
that runs through Uttar Pradesh.
The Mahabharata's most epic tale
in which a simple game of dice
sees Yudhishthira rolling away
his possessions
his kingdom
his brothers
and finally,
his wife, Draupadi.

Bargained and lost to a game of dice
the enraged Draupadi
cursed the river for being
a mute witness to her humiliation,
for watching, silently, not protecting.
She cursed the river, so anyone who

*should drink from it would forever
have a thirst for revenge.*

*Charmanwati doesn't care,
she basks in the glory of the curse,
she winds her way
south through the slopes of the
Vindhyas, Madhya Pradesh,
Rajasthan and Uttar Pradesh.*

*She sings and sighs through
the twists and turns of nature
with her crystal-clear waters,
she bursts with life.*

This curse, *she laughs
through ripples,*
was the greatest gift
ever bestowed upon me,
and if you're ripe for the taking
it's yours.

*But superstition
and black magic rule here
and centuries pass
and wars were waged
blood was shed
revenge was taken
innocents died
and the self-made gods
used force every way they knew how.*

And the women that came after
accepted their fate,
not weak,
they are stronger than you could ever imagine,
you have to be
to endure the hand that life has dealt them.
They pray
wanting more
something better
but chained
accepting this is how it has
simply always been.

That was until Jhano came along.

Witch trials

The year is seventeen ninety-two.
Something sinister is sweeping across India,
whispers of witch trials in Jharkhand
have washed ashore the River Chambal in Uttar Pradesh.
Fingers point,
accusations are made and
the lives of three young women
are put on trial.

The first to be accused is Jhano.
A young woman no longer
calm in the chaos,
and who could no longer
accept her fate.
It was time for her to break free
to find her roar
and wage her own war.

She deserved more than being a silent witness
silently seething on the sidelines
never belonging,
existing for others.
She deserved a choice
a voice
a world she could grab with both hands
knowing that whatever path she wanted to tread
was hers for the taking.

She wanted to knock these self-made gods
off their thrones,
build a new one,
and ride into battle.

Jhano doesn't know what urged her to do it.
What it was that told her enough was enough.
It simply came to her,
a whisper on the wind.

And when she roared,
they said she walked towards the water
they said she was in a trance
they said she disrobed
they said she waded into the river
they said they saw the arms
of the ancient Charmanwati take her
they said they heard the voice of Draupadi whispering to her
the secrets of the past
the secrets to the future.

They said they saw Jhano listen
they said she spoke back in tongues
they said they saw her naked body
bend and break
snap and crack
pulled and pushed.

They said they saw her rise from the water broken
and then disappear into the depths.
They say they saw her emerge recast into
something new
something vile
something dark.

They said she feasted on the decaying corpse of an animal
and then she ran,
she ran on all fours like a beast
disappearing into the ravines.

The accusations were as old as time itself.
A woman had dared to roar,
beating the self-made gods at their own game.
She showed the same brute force
dared to speak up
stood taller
hit harder.
Therefore,
she had to be caught and beaten into submission.
Her mother had warned her,
They will kill you.

I don't care, *said Jhano.*

The self-made gods took Jhano
and her two innocent sisters.

That should send a message, *said one.*

Keep the rest of them quiet
stop them from rising up
and causing a riot, *said the other.*

Might help find me a wife, *said the third.*
The gods reward putting an end to strife.

Yeah, *said the first.*
Yeah, *said the other.*
Yeah, *said the third.*

The self-made gods were happy,
this whole scene was their claim to fame.
They'll go down in history
the keepers of law and order
and saviours from witchcraft.
Oh, how they'll thank us, they laughed.

Villagers gather
they watch
trying to make sense
of this senseless act.

These three women are
not the first to be accused
and they won't be the last.
But they will go down in history as a warning,
should anyone below the self-made gods
wish to roar for more.

The witch doctor plays his games.
Jhano wonders how he thought of them,
from which cruel corner of his dark mind
he birthed these inhumane tricks
from which there's no real escape.
It's all a show
it's all theatre
and here she is in a leading role.

She survives the pain of peppercorns in her eyes
she survives the chillies stuffed down her throat
she survives the beatings
and when they are mad enough
that the three sisters haven't died yet
they are hung from a burning tree.

*Jhano pleads, Spare my sisters.
It's not them you want. It's me.
But the men must send a message.
Some women were excited by Jhano's war
they listened
got on their hands and knees and prayed
vowing to follow.
They saw her as their saviour.*

*There were whispers of an uprising
women started to see their magic
but there were those who liked the old ways
didn't want it challenged,
so, three bodies were taken
to appease, to crush, to shush.*

*Three bodies were hung from a tree
three bodies fought to be free
kicking and screaming
they didn't go without a fight
not until their last dying breath.
Three women tied and tortured
three women with a voice
three women who fought
three women set as an example
three women who were not the first
and not the last
falsely accused and now
gone.*

*But what they didn't see
was Jhano
in her last dying breath*

eyes red raw
body broken
beaten
looking at her daughter, Deeta, and whispering,
You must fight, my daughter. Fight!

Chain reaction

But a daughter
seeing her mother's and her aunts' deaths
can go one of two ways.
Wade into the Chambal River
and get a thirst for revenge
or
she is left frozen in time.
Scarred and scared, she blames her mother
for leaving her in this world
to fend for herself
against the self-made gods.

A motherless daughter is easy prey.
Deeta prays every night
but her prayers go unanswered.
Without the will or wit of her mother
she falls into the life
of the women gone before her
and the women around her.

The self-made gods rise up
more powerful than ever.
The women dim their light,
let the men take control,
forgetting their own magic and power.

Some convince themselves that this is the right way.
They help the men keep control
by teaching their daughters
and their daughters' daughters
that this was the way the gods would want it.
That this way is the only way.

*And the self-made gods sit back and laugh
and say,* Our work is done.

*Jhano's strength is buried deep inside Deeta
but as Deeta grows into a woman her scars run the show.
She still feels their weight.
Unable to release the chains
she passes them on down the line
to her children
and they grow up
and pass the scars
on to their children
and on and on it goes
to the next
and the next
and the next
until we get to*

well, me.

From me to you

If you can believe it
when I came along
I rattled the chains and
pulled the links loose.
Finally, the scars of a daughter
in seventeen ninety-two,
scars that had weighed down
on every other generation
every woman and man
daughter and son
who felt the weight of the chains
and lived with the pain
rose to surface in me,
as strength.
Jhano's strength.

I took those scarred chains
and built my very own suit of armour.
I was brave, I was loud,
I was wild. That's what drew
Shalini and me together.
I saw that it's not only our traumas that define us
but the strength of our ancestors too.

So, you, Rizu,
you have Jhano's blood
running through your veins.
You have her power, her courage.
Take life by the throat
and squeeze every last drop out of it.
Like Jhano before you

be the sun and
the moon!

What about you?
Rizu asks, her eyes wide,
innocent, like when she was a child.

I stumbled. I got scared, I say.
I don't know what I can do now.

It's never too late, Ma.
She takes my hands in hers.
Jhano's strength still runs in you.
If I can be the sun and the moon
then you can be all her stars.

I feel as though a weight has been lifted,
something stirs within me
igniting a fire long forgotten.
For the first time in years
I feel a spark.

And this time, I won't let it fade.
I must keep it alight,
I must stand, I must fight,
not just for me – for Rizu.
So she will never carry the burden I once did,
nor learn to quiet her voice to survive,
nor mistake silence for peace.

Santhal and beyond

I think of the women.
The three bodies that swung
from a tree in seventeen ninety-two.
Eyes red raw
bodies broken
beaten
skin split
cooking in the heat
ready for vultures.

Three women tied and tortured
three women who didn't confess to falsehood
three women set as an example
three women who were not the first
and not the last
falsely accused.

Thinking, is their strength enough to save me
now the whispers and warnings come again.
A history I never asked for stalks me now
and it drags my mother's shadow behind it.

Ghosted

Messages go unanswered,
I'm ignored in the hallways at school,
one day his words were warm,
the next, his silence, cold.

It's like we were never real,
like I never mattered.
I stare at the empty screen,
scrolling past 'goodnights' and 'I miss yous'.

I keep waiting for a sign,
a hint of recognition,
for some comfort
something to ease the pain.

But the truth sits heavy,
his silence screams louder than words.
He's saving himself
letting the blame fall on me,
the burden mine to carry alone.

Life imitating art

Sonu's recording plays on repeat.
The marks on her wrist tell a story
of the bracelet I gave her.
I cursed it, she says,
and now look how it scars her skin.

The comments come flooding in.

Now they say they saw me soaring,
they say I drank blood,
they say I danced bare and wild,
calling forth the devil at night.
They say I tried to conjure his dark power.

I am shattered,
caught up in a whirlwind of denial and hysteria.

Rizu?
My father's face creased with concern.
What's going on?

I have never known how to ask him for help,
I never learned the words,
but in this moment,
he sees me,
the desperation reflected in my eyes.

He gathers me close,
lifting me from the floor,
as the saga spills from my lips.
A tender kiss on my forehead,
he wipes away my tears.
Leave it with me, he asserts.
The promise of protection in his voice.

Dismissed

My parents and I sit in the headteacher's office.
Tension hangs in the air.
Madame Gutherie's computer screen flashes with videos.

This will all blow over, she says
her voice calm, dismissive.
You know how children are.

But this frenzy isn't fading.
It's swelling, darkening.
The words tremble leaving my mother's lips.

Madame Gutherie waves it away.
Probably bots, not even real.
Trust me, the girls will make up
and everything will go back to normal.
She looks at me.
*You **have** apologized to Sonu, Rizu?*

Yes, I say, my voice small.

Well then – she smiles
– Sonu probably needs a little time.
I'll speak with her parents,
don't worry.

And just like that
we are dismissed,
my fate slipping from my grasp,
tossed carelessly into Madame Gutherie's hands.

It is my name

My father pauses at the threshold,
Madame Gutherie,
his voice, taut, restrained.
These aren't just passing words.
There are alarming things being written in these posts,
whispers turning to threats.
They speak of Rizu, they speak of us –
our family tangled in their venomous web.
This isn't just affecting Rizu, it's touching us all.
The accusations have reached my place of work.
This goes beyond a harmless falling-out between friends.
It is serious and you must act.
The hysteria this girl has started is not ending,
it is spreading, Madame Gutherie.
You must rein Sonu in before something truly awful happens.

I'm not sure there is anything –

You must, he insists.
It is our honour.
It is my name.

Just like Abigail

I see Sonu in the hall the following morning
beg to speak with her
but the moment she sees me
she freezes
stares at me
like she's in a trance.

Her eyes flick up
staring at the empty air above
and then she screams
a blood-curdling
spine-chilling scream.

She claws at her throat
fingers frantic, ripping at skin.
Stop it, Rizu, she roars.
Stop it!

Students pause in the hallway
doors swing open
classrooms spill out.
What did you do? they ask.

Me? Nothing, I stutter,
tears on the edge of breaking.
Nothing!

But phones are up in seconds
capturing every scream
a digital swarm waiting to feed.

I thought it was a joke,
the way she stood and stared
eyes glazed over
her hand raised
her finger pointing
like something out of a movie.

Her words start as a whisper,
then rise like a tide.
Witch! she screams, pointing. *Witch!*

I stand, fixed, feeling helpless
my heart pounding in disbelief.
Sonu's gasping,
making out I've blocked her breath,
locked up her lungs.

I scream back,
You've made your point, Sonu,
stop this madness now.
I want to break through the circle of screens
but I know no one is listening.

By the time
the new videos have hit the internet
minds have been made up.
I am a witch.
Like mother, like daughter, they say.
A story to twist and share
a face to point at.

There is nothing I can do but
watch my world fall apart
and spiral out of control.

Spreading

Like a virus
like a fire
like a cancer
like a weed
like a disease

it's taken hold
of hearts and minds
of sense and logic
of reality and truth
it spreads

a whisper in the ear
contaminating homes
turning fable into truth
turning friend into foe
turning sense into stupidity

and fingers point
and lines are drawn
and gangs are formed
and decisions are made
and lies are concocted

and I watch
and listen
and pray

that it passes
vanishes
yesterday's news

but it grows and grows and grows
like a giant before me
a towering beast
a shadow cast only over my world
plunging me into darkness

no running away
no looking back
no wishing it away
no rewind
no fast-forward
past all this
to the good part
to a place I can breathe again

I am stuck
waiting it out
wanting it to be over
wanting to change the past
wanting to run into the future.

Why me?

I watch as Sunny walks the halls untouched.
Like nothing ever happened
while my name is burned into the walls.
I can't help but think, why only me?

We were both there
both in that moment
both guilty of the same thing
a mistake we *both* made
for something we *both* chose.
So why only me?

No fingers point at Sunny
just pats on the back
only one of us paying the price
when it takes –

two to kiss
two to cheat
two to text
two to date
two to embrace.
So why only me?

Why does he get to stay whole
and I'm the one torn apart?

Gaslit

He walks past me in a crowded hallway.
I grab his arm, standing in front of him.

Sunny! Why are you ignoring me?

    I'm not.

You haven't answered any of my messages.

    I didn't get them.

Liar . . .
Can you talk to Sonu? Make her see sense.
Can't you see what she's doing to me?

    It's got nothing to do with me.

How can you say that?
It has everything to do with you.

His eyes dart around him.
Students have stopped in the hall,
Lingering, listening . . .

    I don't even know what you're talking about.

His voice raised,
conscious of those walking by.

What are you talking about?

> *You're stalking me.*
> *That's what I'm talking about.*

What? Sunny . . .

> *You need to leave me alone.*

Why are you saying these things?
You said you loved me.

> *I never said anything like that.*
> *You're delusional.*

That's not true. I don't understand.
Where's the Sunny that held me in his arms all summer?

> *Nothing ever happened between us.*
> *The only thing Sonu saw was you throwing yourself at me.*

Are you being serious?

> *Deadly.*
> *I don't want to get caught up in your drama.*

You're denying what we had?

> *We had NOTHING!*

He shakes,
a bead of sweat
runs down his brow,
colour drains from his face.

Nothing. *Do you hear me?*
Get it through your thick skull
and leave me the hell alone.

My blood runs cold
and once again,
he gets to walk away.

Growing

What started with Sonu,
a spark now a blaze.
Gangs are now forming
in classrooms, the halls,
even online groups.

They see me and scream
their voices tear the air
clutching their stomachs
they writhe and they gasp.
It's her, they'll scream,
she's burning us!

Eyes roll skyward
their hands outstretched
they beg me to stop
to end their visions
to lift the curse they swear
I've laid.

There's nothing I can do
but stand and stare.
Stop, Rizu. Stop!
The words crash round me
I have no power
pleading in silence.

Watch as they collapse in waves
still as death
breath ragged
skin cold.

State of emergency

The teachers are uneasy
parents gripped by fear.
Letters sent
a meeting called.
All eyes on me.
Am I a distraction?
A threat?
Or something darker they can't name?

They fill the school hall
voices tangled
insistent
This must be fixed!
      Our children, their future!
Could she be something more, something dangerous?

Madame Gutherie stands before them
calm, though her anger swells.
Don't be ridiculous, she says.
But they press,
Her mother
      the stories
Gia
      the cult!

None of it's real. Her voice is firm.
This hysteria must stop,
you are worse than the children!
But still, they demand,
their fear louder than reason.

I'm a danger to their children
a curse on the school
I'm not fit for this place.

They
want
me
gone.

The hunt

I'm a witch,
a modern witch!
It's all the rage, don't you know,
a movement sweeping in from the West.

Witches
cults
covens
and now
here I am
a dark-magic queen!

My social media
picked apart, dissected,
every post, every picture,
every object in the background
evidence I've sold
my soul to the devil.

Incense sticks?
Not for prayer – for witchcraft.
That taxidermy rodent I made in science class –
oh, that's for potions.
The childhood doll I loved, cherished –
voodoo, they say.

The accusations
more wild
more absurd
and getting

louder

louder

louder.

A roar
that splits the sky.

I am lost
in a stampede
of wild noise.

Power of three

This is never going to end
I know it, I feel it,
they want blood, Ma, they want blood!

I collapse on to my knees
wanting the ground to swallow me whole.
Crying and shaking,
trying to catch my breath between sobs.

Ma holds me, cradles me
like a small child.
I've got you, she whispers.
I've got you.

I'm not strong enough, Ma...
I'm not
I'm not
I'm not.

Ma holds my face in her hands.
Look at me, Rizu, she says.
I must tell you three things
and I need you to listen.

One.
You, my love, were born with fire in your mouth.
Like a dragon, you roared flames
from the pit of your stomach.
You were burning with rage
the fire of your ancestors in your first flaming breath.

Two.
Rizu, you came into the world covered in scars.
The scars of your ancestors buried into your back,
scars from the fire, the flames, the heat,
the death, the blood, the beat
of hearts stopping.
Their past is your present.
But within these scars are imprints of strength
and courage from the women who fought and endured
*and it runs **deeper** and **stronger** than any scar could.*

Three.
Rizu, I know you have a head full of dreams
and a heart full of desire.
Take that fire and place it in your belly.
Use this madness to fuel it.
Keep it burning
and then use it
to build something new from the ashes.

Out of the ashes

So, they call me a witch,
accusations swirling,
names thrown like confetti,
but here's the twist –
through the darkening chaos,
I see a gentle glow.

My heart might be heavy,
sinking in a flood of fear,
but there's a light breaking through –
my mother, once cloaked in sadness,
now reaches for the sun,

and I feel a subtle transformation,
a connection, as I bathe in her gaze,
witnessing the warmth flood back.

Hysteria

Witch! Witch! Witch!

The words slash through the air.
I'm surrounded in the school hall
with girls and boys
pointing,
clawing
clutching at their bodies,
faces twisted in agony,
doubled over in pain.

Madame Gutherie stands at the front.
Stop this at once! she demands.
I look at her, begging her to help.
Enough is enough!
She tries hard to control
a room full of students but it's too late.

I can see Sonu and the girls
dedicated to their performance.
But when I look around
I see sniggering, the smirks,
the ones going along for fun,
and some, entranced,
caught up in the game.

Stop it! I shout.

Rizu, stop it!
Rizu, stop it!
Rizu, stop it!

Their voices crash against me
layered and frantic.

And then...

One by one
they fall
they writhe
they faint and convulse
shaking like puppets
with strings cut loose.

I scream back.
Stop it! I say.

Stop it!
they repeat,
throwing it back at me
like an echo gone mad,
twisted and warped.

And then,
an almighty roar.
It rises
swelling
deafening,
a sound that crawls under the skin,
a roar that tears through the air
unsettling
unstoppable
like the world itself
is coming undone.

Then,
I feel my legs buckle under me
and a force so fierce pulling me into
another time
another space
another body.

Trial

Witch! Witch! Witch!

The words tear through the air.
The crowd, wild, vicious,
a sea of snarling faces.

I look around.
I'm in a village square.
It feels ancient yet
I know this place
I know this body –
a body that isn't mine,
but somehow it feels unnervingly familiar.

Two women beside me
holding on to me
I look at them –
and know they are my sisters.
Their fear mirrors mine
the chaos, the terror,
we share it.
It flows through us like blood.
Jhano! the younger one says, looking at me.
They are going to kill us!

The crowd closes in, pressing closer
faces twisted with hate.
We scream, we huddle
clutching one another.

But one by one they tear us apart
dragging us across the dirt.
A rope is pulled taut round my neck
my hands bound behind my back.
If this were a dream I would wake.
But I don't.
This is real.
All of it,
too real.

I want to shout but fire rages in my throat.
I choke
I cough
my lungs filled with smoke.

I burn
as flames lick my skin.
I turn to my sisters
their faces battered, bloodied
barely holding on.
Tears blur my vision
but I am not weak.

And there in the crowd
a young girl
terrified
alone
with no one to shield her from this horror.
And although I've never seen her before
I know who she is.
I am Jhano and this is my daughter.
I gather the last of my strength
my voice torn but fierce,
You must fight, my daughter. Fight!

Reality

The world settles back into place.
I open my eyes
everything blurs.
My throat raw
a desert in my mouth
I gasp
my lungs constricting.

Madame Gutherie looms over me
her voice emerging from the fog.
Come with me.

Her hand is firm on my arm
pulling me upright.
The world sways
legs, shaking
knees, weak.
I'm stumbling,
half carried, half dragged.

Around me, bodies,
classmates strewn across the floor
limp as rag dolls.
I'm forced to step over them
one by one
as Madame Gutherie
keeps pulling me away
both of us escaping from the scene.

Prisoner

I have no choice
but to stay at home
like a prisoner.
I am locked away
for my own safety
they say.

I am the Delhi schoolgirl
practising witchcraft
cursing her classmates.

Just like you, Ma,
history repeats.
I don't want this any more.
I'm scared, Ma,
I'm scared thinking about what they might do.
Can I leave the school? Please.
Start again somewhere new?

Remember what I told you, Rizu.
You were born with a strength
no one can match.

Don't say that, Ma!
I'm not strong!
I can't be who you want me to be.

She holds my face in her hands.
I ran, Rizu.
I stayed silent.
It didn't work.
We'll brave the winds together,
no matter how wild it gets, I'm here with you.
This will all be over soon.
I promise.

FOUR

A family business

Lalu is a witch doctor.
He believes he is a good man,
a godly man,
fulfilling his godly duty
like that of all the great men who came before him.
Putting an end to evil
and upholding all that is good and decent in society.

He wakes up that morning
and goes through his daily routine
like every other day.

The morning is hot
and he's sweating again by the time he's put on his clean clothes
and sighs at the wet patches under his arms.
He sits for a moment and thinks about the young woman he's about to see,
and the family, the man, who has employed him, Naresh Jain.
A very rich and powerful man – he's happy with the assignment,
a first for him, he has never been called upon by such a person.
He thinks about the evil that may have possessed the girl
who has cursed Naresh's daughter
and the tools he might need.

He looks around his room –
something extra, he thinks.
From what he's heard and seen, this girl –
Rizu – is possessed by a particularly dark force,
a force stronger than anything he might have seen before.

He takes some clay and matches,
puts them in his bag

along with parcels of rice
chillies, snake blood, rope and a knife.
He looks in his bag one more time
and once he's happy with his lot
he closes it and walks out of his home
ready for a long train journey to Delhi.
With any luck he should be there by late afternoon,
ready to rid the world of another witch.

A poppet

Sonu can't walk.
They say I took a doll,
stuck needles into its spine,
and now look at her,
her legs refusing to move.

She sits in a wheelchair,
carried from bed to bathroom,
even the sceptics
believe the whispers are true,
I am the monster they claim.

There's evidence –
a doll in my room,
button eyes staring,
Sonu swears she saw me,
with needles and pins,
waving my hands, casting spells.

The air burns with accusations.

What will happen next?
Will they drag me into a trial of terror?
I can't escape this feeling –
the walls are closing in,
dark clouds are gathering.

It's only a matter of time
before the mob are at my door,
drawn in by their own fears.
I feel it.
They're coming for me.

Naresh Jain

Desperation

Any father would have done the same.
I watch my daughter,
once vibrant, now fading,
lost in a world of pain.

I see her hurt on screens,
her screams echoing in my mind.
What am I to do –
sit back and do nothing?
What kind of father would that make me?

This is something new,
a darkness is creeping in,
beyond the reach of normal law,
something deeper, more sinister.
There is evidence,
I'm seeing it, unfolding before my eyes.

Some call it backward thinking,
but when it's your own flesh and blood,
you can't ignore the truth,
you must take action.

Some say she is lying,
that my daughter is hurt, embarrassed,
out for revenge.
But I know her,
I know her heart,
she would never –
that's not who she is.

And now?
Now she can't walk.
This is no act,
this requires resolution,
help from those who understand this world,
the origins of dark magic,
the evil lurking within.

This girl, Rizu,
she has cast her spell,
and she must be stopped.

Whatever the witch doctor conjures
is his own affair.
I'm just a father,
desperate to save his daughter.

The Hunting Pack

Reckoning

We gather, we grow,
a fierce, frenzied force.
We stalk,
we strike,
on our vengeful course.

We move as one,
our whispers rise,
Rizu now in our sight.
This girl will face the night.

Our hearts thrum with fury,
adrenaline ignites,
some seek justice,
some crave a fight.

Some thrive on the tale,
on the whispers and dread,
while the wolves gather round,
her fate being read.

Our breath comes in rasps,
a chilling, eager sigh,
our pack, closing in,
there's nowhere for this witch to fly.

In the dark we encroach,
our hunger now a fire,
for justice, for vengeance,
our primal desire.

A pact forged in darkness,
where right meets wrong,
in the heart of the hunt,
we'll be fierce, we'll be strong.

A twist

Just when I thought the storm had passed
clouds roll back, twice as fast.

I thought I'd felt it all
but there's always more, another fall.

I'm the voodoo queen, with my dolls in a line.
Sonu can't walk, a mark of my design.

Here it comes, another blow, another twist
never did I think it would ever come to this.

Wolves at the door

They've emerged from the shadows,
the whole gated community,
a ravenous pack,
eyes gleaming with a thirst for blood and truth,
pulsing palpitating pressuring.
They circle, closing in,
the sound of their breathing
as sharp as knives in the air.
I feel the weight of it all.

Sonu is wheeled in,
her body frail,
words barely a whisper,
a flicker of fear across her pale face.
I wonder,
does she regret how far this has gone?

Does anyone possess the doll?
The witch doctor's voice cuts through the murmur.
You must ask the girl, Rizu,
Sonu's father declares,
his gaze a stone,
fixated on me like a hawk.
She's the one using it, it belongs to her.

I don't have a doll.
I haven't owned a doll since I was a little girl.
I feel my voice rising, frantic, desperate.
Can't you see? Sonu is faking!
Silence falls, heavy as a shroud.

Silence, girl! he barks,
his eyes hardening, hunting for secrets.
Where are you hiding it?

I'm not hiding anything!
Defiance burns in my chest
yet my voice is small, weak.
He turns to Jaya.
You. Go find this doll,
he commands.

I've never seen a doll in this house.
Her voice quakes,
her hands shake.
She looks at me,
eyes wide with fear,
desperate to help
but lost in the chaos,
helpless to know how.

Sonu, Preeti, Mia, Tanya,
pointing at me, eyes wild.
Why are you doing this? Sonu shrieks,
her gaze cutting through me.
Their hands clutch their chests, gasping
as if something grips them from within.

What is it you see? the witch doctor demands,
his tone heavy, relentless.
Speak the truth, my child.

Something awful, Sonu whispers, trembling.
Something awful, the girls echo,
a chorus of rising dread.

Sonu, stop it! I shout, my voice splintering.
Sonu, stop it! they cry in unison like a spell taking root.
Stop it! I scream, my heart hammering in my throat.
Stop it! they cry back, a cacophony of despair,
rising, melding, into one primal wail.

The witch doctor turns,
piercing gaze fixed on me.
What are you doing to them? he accuses,
as if I pull the strings to their torment.

Nothing! I plead. *I'm not doing anything!*

These girls have gone mad!
My mother's voice slices through the chaos,
drenched in disbelief.
A joke spun too far!
Surely you can't believe this?
She scans the gathering wolves,
searching for reason.
I can't take any more,
desperation grips me as I rush to Sonu
launching myself at her,
Get up! Get up, you liar!
I drag her from the chair,
her body, limp,
collapsing to the floor.

My daughter wouldn't lie!
Sonu's mother shrieks.
I believe what I see.
She cradles Sonu,
lifting her up into the chair,
fear twisting her features.
Something must be done, she insists.

Like mother, like daughter,
someone mutters.
The words sting.
The pack presses in,
their gazes fixed,
an unyielding circle of accusation.
Desperation hardens my mother's face.
See sense! she cries,
but reason has fled.

The wolves want answers,
their hunger insatiable,
sifting through every misfortune,
every whisper of ill fate,
every illness, every failed venture,
every broken marriage,
and have come to one conclusion –
someone must be guilty
someone has called this evil forth.

My mother's laugh echoes,
wild and broken,
You've lost your minds!
But the pack won't listen.

The witch doctor steps forward,
his patience worn thin.
Is it both of them? he demands,
eyes glinting with resolve.
Mother and daughter?

Probably, the wolves whisper,
their eyes locked on us,
hungry for justice.
They close in,
their breath a heat against our skin.

We are trapped.
They are upon us now.

Desperation

It was the housekeeper. It was Jaya!

The words leap from my father's lips,
his face contorted in disbelief,
an accusation torn from him
before he could even make sense of it.

He stares at Jaya,
her breath caught, frozen in the dark
until the pack drag her forward
into the circle, with us –
my mother, my father and me.

No, Raaj! my mother cries
her voice breaking through panic.

No! I scream, my voice shattering.

It's true, it's her, it's Jaya! my father insists,
his voice breaking with fear.

Raaj, what are you saying? my mother begs him.

I am drowning in shock,
paralysed by the terror in Jaya's eyes.
The silent plea that lingers between us –
Don't say that. Don't bring her into this, I say.

Who is it, then? The witch doctor's voice cuts the air.
Your daughter? Your wife? Or the housekeeper?

The wolves wait for blood.

My father falls to his knees.
The food she makes, it sickens us, she . . . she . . .
His words fail him, his shame too great,
she makes advances, seductive . . .
A cry tears through his chest.

That's not true! Jaya screams, her voice raw.
She looks at me and my mother
eyes wide, pleading.

She's telling the truth, I beg you,
don't do this, don't bring Jaya into this –
but my voice is inaudible in the commotion.

Meena has been ill since Jaya came into this house.
She wants to replace her. She wants to . . .
I watch my father break, unable to speak the words,
but we all feel them, hanging in the air, laced with lies.

The witch doctor steps forward.
Is this true? He grips Jaya by the face,
fingers pressing into her skin.
Have you been casting black magic?
Have you cursed the family?
Do you wish to take Meena's place?

No! Jaya chokes,
her words crushed by terror.
It's not true, it's not.

It is true! my father interjects,
as if trying to convince himself.
She told me! She said she could be . . .
she said she could be a better wife than Meena.

The witch doctor's eyes widen with the thrill of a catch.
What kind of spirit takes you over?
Who did you summon?
He draws a blade, quick and brutal,
and slices through the skin of Jaya's palms.
She shrieks, a cry that shatters the fragile air.

I lunge to save her,
throwing myself on to her small body,
yanking her from the witch doctor's grip.
My mother rushes in,
both of us wild, hearts racing,
desperate to pull her to safety,
to tear her from this hold before it's too late.

You can save her! I cry to my father.
You can save her! I plead,
my voice a lifeline thrown to Sonu.
Both hang their heads,
unable to face the truth.

Sonu, a girl sinking in her own tide of vengeance,
my father, a man spiralling into his own madness.
One desperate to preserve pride,
the other clinging to the remnants of family.

Last chance

The pack is barking,
their snarls low and dangerous.
They don't know what to believe any more.
Creeping closer, through dense, suffocating heat
sweating and salivating.

I scream, *It's not true!*

But the witch doctor shoots back,
Well, if it's not her, it's you!

Panic takes hold.
How can I save this life
without offering up my own?
I look at Sonu,
her eyes flicker,
full of doubt and hesitation.
You can stop this, my voice desperate.
You have the power to end it.

I search her face
trying to read what lies beneath.
She seems small now
almost shrinking in the chaos
a puppet caught in the grip of something
she can no longer control.
Revenge gone too far
or maybe still not far enough.
I can't tell.

Please, Sonu, I beg,
before someone really gets hurt.
But Sonu doesn't look at me,
she simply slips back, away from the pack.

Jaya

Scapegoat

I run.
I am caught.
The pack grabs hold
pulling, tearing,
fingers like claws.

I scream
the sound ripping from my throat
wishing the earth to open up
allowing me to slip through the cracks.

If only I could burrow deep,
run through the earth –
bloodied, broken
but breathing.
Alive.

I will not die today!
I scream it so loud
my chest aches.
I will not die today!

Maybe my mother
miles away
will hear it.
Maybe she'll fly to me,
take me in her arms,
pull me from their grasp
and save me.

I will not die today!

Sonu

Regret

I never meant for it to go this far.
I only wanted to be seen,
for my wounds to matter,
for the weight of my pain to be felt.
The anger was power once,
a flame I could hold
but now the fire is wild,
uncontrollable.
I lit the match
but I can't put out the blaze.

I watch her,
pleading for mercy.
I will not die today! she screams.
God, I want to take it back
to undo it all.
I thought revenge would end the ache
but this isn't justice.
It's dark,
devouring me
as it's devouring her.

A lie gone too far
and I'm too small
and it's too late
to turn back.

Raaj

Misguided

Any father would have done the same.
What am I to do –
sit back and do nothing?
What kind of father would that make me?

I had no choice.
The pack is closing in.
Eyes wild, fists clenched,
and Rizu
my daughter
my flesh and blood
is in their sights.

I see the fire in their eyes
and their thirst for blood . . .
When Jaya's name left my mouth
it felt like betrayal
but also, a release.

What kind of man am I?
I have to believe
it was the only way,
I've done what any father would do.
But deep down rot settles in
as I hear her scream,
I will not die today!

> Whatever the witch doctor conjures
> is his own affair.
> I'm just a father,
> desperate to save his daughter.

Witness

They rip us from Jaya,
the pack prowls, tears, pulls –
their claws clutch at my arms,
holding us hostage,
forcing our eyes to the horror.
Jaya!
I thrash, I lurch, I scream her name,
but there are too many of them.
Their hands clamp me down,
their snarls smother my fight.

None of this makes sense.
This isn't real,
It can't be real.

You came for me! I howl.
So take me!

The witch doctor's hand, stone-hard,
cinches round Jaya's slender neck.
A noose of judgement, cruel and cold.
Rizu, help. Jaya's voice,
barely escaping her throat,
her palms pressed together, a prayer for mercy.
But there's no mercy here.

I lunge again, wild, feral,
my mother too.
Get off her! my mother shrieks.
But the witch doctor shoves her aside,
as the wolves swarm me,
fangs at my feet,
dragging me away.

The witch doctor chants,
his voice rising with the hunger of a beast closing in.
Leave her body, demon!
His growl splits the air.
I can feel your presence!
And the wolves join the chorus,
a cacophony of chaos,
fuelling the fire.

She can't breathe! I wail,
my voice breaking,
my chest bursting with a sob so raw
it tears at my throat.
But no one hears.
No one listens.

Jaya's breath falters,
as the witch doctor continues undeterred,
hands pressed to her mouth and throat,
his grip too strong –

the world tilts.
I claw at the earth,
my voice a splintered scream,
He's killing her! STOP! PLEASE!

I turn to my parents.
My mother, with wildfire in her eyes,
thrashes in my father's unrelenting hold,
her screams slicing through the frenzy.
But my father – silent, still –
a statue in this theatre of madness.

Jaya fights to speak
but the witch doctor tightens his grip,
an iron vice, ruthless,
as Jaya fights for breath,
fighting for her life.

She looks at me, lips trembling,
her voice a shattered whisper,
Rizu . . .
Her eyes wide, wild,
clinging to life,
to me,
to hope.

I feel a pressure building in my throat,
something loud,
something primal.
I want to roar,
I want to rip apart the air,
to tear the world open,
but all that escapes my lips
is a broken, pitiful,
I'm so sorry. I'm so sorry.

And then the world stills.
Her breath fades.
Her body falls.
The witch doctor lets her go,
and she folds like a rag doll,
limp and motionless
her spark snuffed out.

No.
It's a whisper, then a howl.
No, no, no, NO!

I throw myself to the ground,
grasp her limp body,
shake her,
beg her,
Wake up! Jaya, please, wake up!

Sometimes the demon inside is too strong,
he says, cold as ice
and the pack believe him.
They swallow the lie like it's holy,
it's easier this way,
cleaner, better for everyone.

A scapegoat.
A sacrifice.

I wonder –
will they wake tomorrow and remember?
Will they feel an ounce of regret?
Or will they think themselves lucky it was the servant girl,
because servant girls are easy to forget.

The Pack Awakens

Speak no evil

The air stills –
silence heavy as stone.
The frenzy fades,
and in its place –
an empty void.

The witch doctor's voice cuts through:
Sometimes the demon inside is too strong.
We nod, wooden,
clinging to his words,
a murmur ripples through us,
a wave of half-hearted agreement.
Yes.
The demon.
It was her fault.
It was never ours.

And yet –

Our hands itch.
Our breath feels too loud.
The dirt under our nails seems darker,
grittier, heavier somehow.
And though we know
we're supposed to feel cleansed,
whole,
safe –
we don't.

Someone clears their throat,
a cough to break the quiet.
We scatter like leaves,
our feet dragging,
our heads down.

And yet –

Her absence clings to us.

We tell ourselves it's nothing.
It will pass.
It always does.

Won't it?

And yet –

In the pit of our stomachs,
something churns,
and deep inside,
something twists.

Echoes of you

I hold Jaya's hands –
still warm, still soft,
but her warmth is
fading like the last light
of a dying star.

I'm sorry, I whisper,
the words breaking,
fragile as glass.
I'll never forgive myself for not saving you.

My tears fall,
carving rivers down my face,
drowning in the memories.

*Our breakfasts, stolen moments
in the quiet corner of the kitchen,
away from the noise of parties,
away from the suffocating smiles
of the too-perfect relatives.*

*Your stories still echo,
your laughter,
your voice softening as you spoke of home.
You were my home.*

*I'll miss your laugh,
your patience when I stumbled,
your courage when I couldn't find mine.
I'll miss how you saw me –
the me no one else bothered to see.*

*You were the only one
who ever really knew me.*

*Now, there's no one.
No one to share the small joys,
no one to anchor me
when the world spins too fast.*

I clutch her hands as if to bind us,
to hold her here,
and stop her from slipping away.

You're gone.

The words stay stuck in my throat,
and in this hollow, aching moment,
I know –
I've lost my only friend.

The weight of silence

The weight of her murder
presses against me,
dense, unshakable.

My mother folds, beside herself,
hands shaking as she reaches for the phone.
We should call the police.

My father is faster,
snatching the phone from her grasp.
No one is calling the police.

We should tell her family,
my mother weeps, her sobs uncontrollable.

Tell them what? Tell them what, Meena?
My father paces wild circles around the room.
We can't tell anyone.

Anger ricochets between them,

Don't be ridiculous, Raaj!

                      Do you know how many years you'd get for murder?

So what? We cover this up?

                      Yes!

Who are you?

                      I'm the one saving this family, Meena!

Shut up! Both of you, shut up!
My voice strikes like a whip.
I glare at my father,
my gaze burning into him.
Look at her! I scream.
Look at what you did!

He stares at Jaya's body,
her stillness louder than the chaos.
I had no choice. His voice hollow,
his eyes sinking into regret.
That could have been you.

I hold Jaya fiercely,
her warmth escaping through my fingers.
I will her to breathe,
to blink,
to laugh,
to tell me this is some cruel joke.

But the stillness is unbroken,
the silence grows heavier,
a noose coiling round us all.

Discarded

She's still warm –
her body concealed in a sheet,
silence heavy, suffocating,
as our driver, Santosh, carries her from the house.

I can't bear to watch.
He bundles her into a car,
takes her somewhere
far from here –
a secluded place outside the city,
hidden from prying eyes.

I hate how easy it is,
how people like us
brush away the blood,
the truth,
and move on unscathed –
as if her life was nothing more
than a blemish to be erased.

What do I do with this weight in my chest,
the tremor inside my ribs?
My father –
his hands stained,
his face flooded with guilt,
his voice shuddering with *I did it for you*.
And yet,
it was his fear, his accusation,
his voice that sent her to her death.

And Sonu –
Sonu lit the match.
She started the fire
that scorched us all.
She walks free, hands clean,
while my father bears the burden,
and I bear the rage.

A taste for revenge coats my tongue,
bitter and stinging,
as something primal, feral,
begins to claw its way out of my chest.

My body burns with it,
my veins vibrate with fury . . .
Until the world spins again,
spilling me into another time,
another space,
another body.

The messenger

You must fight, my daughter. Fight!

This time I am the girl watching,
not the woman hanging,
and I am frightened and alone
without a family to call my own.
I'm standing, staring eyes fixed
on a horror I don't want to see.

I'm glad you called.
A voice speaks to me from within the crowd.
When I look up, I see her,
the woman from the mirror
the woman from my dreams.

You? I say.

> *Yes, me. Who else were you expecting?*

I . . . I'm not sure I was expecting anyone.

> *But you called.*

I did?

> *Yes.*

When?

> *You've been calling me since the day you were born.*
> *Sorry it's taken me so long. I was waiting for the right moment.*

Who are you?

> *Have you still not figured that out? . . . I'm Jhano.*
> *I know you've heard of me.*

Jhano? The one hanging from . . .

> *How I died doesn't matter.*
> *It's how I lived.*
> *I was born of fire,*
> *I roared into this world, just like you.*
> *I answered the call when it came*
> *and although my life was cut short*
> *oh, how I roared.*
> *Now, will you?*

I don't understand.

> *I was the last to answer.*
> *Since then no one has listened,*
> *but you, Rizu, you are different.*
> *That's why you're here.*
> *That's why you can see me.*

I look up at the tree
and then back at her.

> *Heroes don't always get a happy ending.*
> *But it's a different time.*
> ***Your*** *story will be different.*
> *Can't you feel it?*

I shake my head. No. Sorry.

She leans in. *Because you refuse to believe it.*

Why now? I ask.
Why all the visions, the voices?
Why am I here?

She smiles. *Because you called.*

You keep saying that but I didn't,
I blurt out, unable to hide the irritation in my voice.

> *Not with your voice, but with your heart.*
> *You have been aching to roar since you were small.*
> *I have seen how you look at the painting above your parents' bed.*
> *I know you long to embody the fierce, feminine Draupadi,*
> *how you want her fire and fury for yourself.*
> *You're old enough to take on the challenge now, Rizu.*
> *It's time to stop pretending.*

I'm not who you think I am.

> *Yes, you are. I know you.*
> *We are the same.*

We're not.
I'm scared
I'm a stupid schoolgirl
I'm a coward.

> *You underestimate yourself.*

I'm just being honest.

You felt the heat in your blood, didn't you?

Yes.

*You felt the pulse of injustice
coursing through your veins.*

Yes.

*Then hold on to that.
You were born of fire, Rizu.
Now burn.*

Born of fire

When I open my eyes,
their faces hover above me –
my mother gripping my shoulders,
my father looming over me, silent, still.

I hear the pulse, distant but steady,
the beat of my heart pounding
against the hollow ache in my chest.
The heat rises, slow and curling,
coiling in my blood.

It's here.
The fire she spoke of.
I can feel it – but it scares me.
It's a weight I can't carry.

What would Jaya have done?
Her laughter haunts the silence,
her courage feels like a rebuke.
I see her face, her kindness, her trust.
I see her fall –
and my failure burns brighter than any fire.

I clasp my hands against my chest,
as if I can smother it,
this roar clawing to be free.
But I can't let it out.
I don't have her strength.
I don't have her fire.
Jhano believes in me, but she's wrong.

The heat pulses in my veins,
a wild force desperate to rise.
But I turn away.
I swallow it down.
This is not who I am.
This is not who I can be.

I meet my mother's eyes –
she's afraid of what she sees in me,
and so am I.
I see my father's silence, his regret,
his weight pressing on us all.
He says it was for me,
but I didn't want his protection.
I didn't want any of this.

Jhano's voice whispers,
Born of fire, now burn.
But I'm not like her.
I never was.
I'm not ready.
I'll never **be** ready.

So I let the fire smoulder,
let it cool to embers.
I bury it deep, because I know
I haven't got what it takes.

And as the weight of grief pulls me down,
I close my eyes and let the fire fade.

Back and forth

It's late.
I sit, splintered,
deep into night,
my eyes fixed on the screen,
flickering, hypnotic,
staring not seeing,
lost in loops of thought.

I search for a way,
for answers buried in the dark,
this 'calling', the meaning,
for the right path to follow.

What am I meant to be?
Where do I go from here?
The questions spin,
whirling and churning.
I ask the silence –

Nothing.

Born of fire, she says.
Born to burn.
What does that even mean?

I'm not strong,
not fierce,
not the girl
she thinks I was born to be.
I am small,
lost,
nothing but the weight of my mistakes,
the weight of blood spilled.

Jaya, I whisper. *Jaya.*
If I hadn't gone with Sunny,
if I hadn't . . .
But I did.
I did and now you're gone.
I'm the cause,
I'm so, so sorry.

I bury my face in my pillow,
drowning out the sobs,
sorrow soon turning to rage,
it flares inside me,
hot, burning.

Jhano, are you there?
I ask the empty air.

A quest

You're making me work hard,
Jhano says with a smile.

Tell me, I beg,
just tell me what I'm supposed to do.

She steps closer,
and the air feels different,
charged.
*Your name, Rizu,
it means mighty.*

I don't feel mighty, I say.
I feel small, worthless.

Your mother, she continues,
*she was meant for great things,
but her path twisted,
she stopped listening to the call,
trapped herself between these marble walls,
and so, like her, you now walk a different path.
But it doesn't have to be that way, Rizu.
You were never meant for this life.
This life of marble walls and empty rooms.
You, Rizu, were always meant for more.
You were meant for the open road,
for the wild, for the storms and the stars.
Everything that has happened, Rizu,
has been pulling you, drawing you here,
to this very moment and sometimes, in life,
if you do not jump with the freedom of your own will,*

if you hesitate, if you wait too long,
the world will shift beneath you,
and life will push you from the edge.
Leave, Rizu, she says, softly but firm.
Leave this cage
and go see who you can really become.
Go see the strength you never knew you had.
Use this dark hour and be a catalyst for change.
Go, before it's too late.

Her words sink into me.
You have a choice, Rizu –
her eyes lock with mine –
you can choose to be something different.

How can I be someone else? I say.
Someone strong,
when all I've known is weakness?

The weight of weakness

How can I stand alone
when I look in the mirror each morning and wonder,
Who am I allowed to be today?
When I dare not change my hair,
when every strand feels
like a decision I'm too afraid to make.

How can I walk tall
when I don't even dare to wear lipstick
that might make me feel like someone else?
When every small step outside what's *safe*
feels like breaking everything I've been shown to be.

How do you step into strength
when you don't even trust yourself to dress for the day,
when every choice feels like a war
between who I'm told to be and who I'm afraid to become?

Is this weakness?
This hesitation,
this constant bending,
too scared to shine,
living in the shadow of myself
because it's safer
than the noise of my own choices?

Maybe,
just maybe,
weakness is the prison
I've built with my own hands,
brick by brick,
with every *no* I've said to myself,
every *I can't*,
every time I've stayed small.

Maybe it's time to shatter the walls.
Maybe it's time to be someone else,
someone I don't recognize,
someone who dares to be different
someone who isn't afraid to be *seen*.
Maybe it's time to look inside
and find the real me.

An answer

But where am I supposed to go? I ask.
The question lingers, unanswered
until the TV flickers to life.

Echoes of three sisters.
Village. Uttar Pradesh.
Shalini.
Her gang.
Justice.
I sit up,
listening,
watching.

Shalini moves with the force of a storm,
charisma crackling in every breath,
a force that pulls every eye towards her.
Every word she speaks is a command,
articulate, unstoppable.
She answers with the certainty of someone
born to stand in the light,
born to change the world.

And when she's done,
when her voice fades into silence,
she looks directly at the lens –
and then through it,
through the screen,
into me.
Her gaze hits like fire.

You ready, Rizu? she asks.

The penny drops

Shalini?
Ask for her help?
Why would someone like her
help someone like me?

You'll see, Jhano says.
Actually, I think you could both
help each other.

And then, just like that, she's gone.
Vanished.
But her presence still lingers,
and in the silence,
a spark ignites,
a glimmer of understanding,
something stirring inside me,

a hint of courage
of possibility
I never knew was there.

Fire

It's here.
The fire she spoke of.
It burns in me now,
a slow steady roar
I can no longer ignore.

I feel it in my veins
coursing through every breath,
a force too wild
too strong to turn away from.

I spy on my parents.
I see my mother's fear,
my father's silent shame.
I know I can no longer stay.
Another path is calling,
another path that is mine.

Defiance

No, she says, it's not safe.
It's dangerous for a daughter
daring to defy the dark alone.
You hear the stories every day,
young women are prey.
It's a predator's playground.

Look around, I say,
a murder under this roof.
How do you mask that mess?
How do we explain away death
with dinner and dresses?

I did what I had to do.
If not, that would have been you,
your blood on the carpet.
He looks at me like it's the truth
but I know it's not.

That's a lie.
You know that man would never
have put his hands round my throat.
You know that if he had,
you would have wrestled him to the ground.
*You know that **if** he had killed me*
there would be hundreds of police here now arresting everyone.
My death would see justice being carried out.
You know that you let this happen.
Everyone let this happen.
My voice breaks.
***I** let this happen.*

And we know why,
we know the truth,
we know how this all works.
People like Jaya, their lives mean less,
easy to dispose of, easy to forget.
You know why you said her name, just admit it.
Her death would end all this, clean, easy.
What did you think would happen afterwards?
That we would all go back to playing happy families?
It doesn't work like that.

My heart hammers out of my chest,
words leaping from my lips
before I can catch my breath.

I can't stay here.
I won't.
I can't look at you . . .
you disgust me.

Rizu, he says, pleading,
please don't say that.

It's true, I continue.
You are as much the murderer as that witch doctor.
I can't stay. This house, this city,
stained with its secrets, is tainted now.
This isn't my home any more.

I say, *I'm going.*
She says, *Where?*
Shalini, I say with defiance.
She laughs.
What's so funny? I spit,
as she calls me crazy.

Crazy? I say. *Look at this madness,
this blood-painted palace.*

She brushes away my words,
You don't even know where she lives!

Now I'm laughing,
phone flashing,
fingers dancing,
showing her how easy it is
to find a ghost
in this grid of glass.
*There's a train in an hour.
I'll be there by midday.
I'm packed, I'm ready.
You can't stop me.*

*Oh no you don't.
I'm not losing you, Rizu!*
She grabs, claws at my arm,
we wrestle, caught in a chaos of despair.
What about school, Rizu?

What about it? I can miss a few days, weeks –

Weeks! Your life is here, Rizu! With your family.
She looks at my father, demands, *Stop her!*
But he's a ghost now,
silent, standing, staring at bloodstains.

I need to leave, Ma,
so I can find out what it is I need to do,
who it is I need to be.

Ma screams and shakes us both
desperate to drag us back from the brink
but we are all coming apart
thread by fragile thread
hanging without a harness.

In the back of my throat
there's a scream waiting
a piercing sound
a rage rattling in its cage
a fire begging for freedom.

I catch my reflection
see flames flickering behind my eyes.
I've stayed silent,
scared, small for too long, Ma.
You told me I had strength
you told me to burn bright
build something new from the ashes.

Not like this
*not with **her***
not with Shalini.

If not now, when?
I've made up my mind.
You have to let me go.

With one hand she digs her nails
into the flesh of my upper arm
determined to keep me from running.
With the other she scratches at my father's face
desperate to wake him out of his trance.

As her nails cut my skin
waves of rage travel through my body.

From the earth beneath my feet
something deep and primal
is releasing a power locked within.

I open my mouth, unleashing an otherworldly sound
and with it breaking centuries of chains.

I am between multiple worlds now
as I rip the room apart

releasing

    my

        ROAR.

Burn baby burn

With no clue, no way to see,
I'll face my fear, set myself free.
No answers, no guide, no light at all,
but still, I'll stand, and answer the call.

FIVE

The journey begins

And so it starts.
Our hero has answered the call.
Soon she'll start to question everything she's ever known.
Turning her back on a life she once lived,
she'll settle into a new way of being,
speak in ways her tongue is not used to,
build her body in ways she could never have imagined,
build an army, travelling through this world and the next,
slaying gods
and destroying their world.

Into the unknown

Delhi clings to my skin as I step out of the door.
Heat shimmers on the pavement
the city buzzing under the weight of the rising sun.
I hail a tuk-tuk to the station.
The streets pulse with activity
as we wind through rivers of traffic and faces.

I don't look back, I can't.
The ache of leaving
and the fear of what lies ahead
twist inside me.

The train to Kota is late.
Like everything here,
slow and heavy with heat.
I board, squeezing through narrow aisles,
looking for a place to breathe.

The seats are hard, packed with strangers.
They stare,
I feel as though I'm wearing my rich-girl upbringing
like a badge. I've never travelled in third class before.
My discomfort is obvious.

A prickle of unease creeps up my spine.
The weight of my backpack suddenly unbearable.
The reality of the journey hits me –

I am alone.

No driver, no carefully planned itinerary,
no familiar voices guiding me.
The noise of the train swells around me.
I swallow hard.
The courage I felt when leaving has dulled into something else –
I feel unsettled. I try to steady myself, but fear still lingers.

Beside me a woman cradles her crying child,
a man sleeps, snoring gently.
I sit, face pressed against the window,
feeling the vibration of the train's heartbeat
as Delhi fades behind me in smog and heat.
My mind, crammed, crowded like the station
and moments I'll never outrun, no matter how far I go.
I feel light-headed,
What am I doing on this train?
What do I think is going to happen?
What do I think Shalini can even do?
Who will I uncover beneath my own mask?

The train rattles on,
cutting through fields and villages,
passing endless rows of crops,
bent backs in the distance,
harvesting in the scorching sun.

The heat grows worse as I move south,
sweat running down my spine,
the air in the train growing stale.
Vendors call out at stops
selling water, chai
and samosas wrapped in newspaper.

Outside the land turns dry
the colours of the earth deepening.
Children run barefoot along the tracks
chasing the train with laughter.

Kota grows closer,
its promise hanging
like a mirage on the horizon.

But as I step off the train
and into a new city
I feel the weight of the journey
settle into my bones.

I stand on the platform
surrounded by faces
yet I feel completely alone.
The train departs,
a blur of heat and noise
fading behind me,
the rhythm of it still beneath my feet
carrying me to whatever comes next.

No turning back

I think of all I'm leaving behind.
Shadows of absent parents,
friends twisted into foes,
a life draped in designer silks.

Will I be missed?
Or will this whole saga be forgotten?
When will I return?
Who will I return?

Mostly I think of Jaya.
Jaya whose laughter was my lantern,
whose warmth protected my aching heart.

I still feel a tug of war,
between the call of the unknown
and the chains of a place that broke my family
and took my friend.

Am I ready for this journey?
Doubt whispers in my ear,
indecision coils around my steps.
What am I chasing?
What if I find nothing?
What if I learn I am – nothing?

I feel a pang of anxiety,
I think of turning back,
back into the station and racing home.
I pause for a moment, my feet uncertain.

No.

I put my hand on my heart
determined to steady its racing beat.
I can't turn back, not now.
I've started on this journey,
I've come this far,
I might as well walk further.
Maybe, just maybe, I'll become
something more than the echoes of my past.

So, I step forward.
Not with confidence,
but with the weight of necessity,
seeking to discover if I can
become more than I am.

Meena

Spirals

The walls close in.
We vow to bury ourselves in silence,
to suffocate under the weight
of what happened here.

Raaj collapses near the bloodstained rug,
fingers trembling, tracing the gruesome outline.
It's all my fault.

I can't speak.
I can't tell him it's not.
Jaya's life mattered,
she was no less than Rizu.
Tears threaten to spill
as I think there could have been another way
out of this madness.

I didn't think it would end like this.
Words spill out between sobs.
I'm so sorry.

It's done. It's over.
I clutch at my chest,
swallowing the scream building inside.

We sit on opposite sides
of the bloodstained rug,
the air heavy with the scent of loss.
Our love, once whole,
now fractured and worn.
Looking at him, it's hard to know
if it can ever be restored.

They say life works in spirals.
I never expected that mine
would twist so cruelly
where another life
is taken.

Arrival

The ground beneath my feet feels
unfamiliar, charged with anticipation.
I repeat the address to the driver
and the taxi surges forward,
tearing through the labyrinth of streets.

Ahead looms the house – imposing yet simple –
perched high above the Chambal, the river winding below.
I feel like it's protecting the house, some ancient force.
Its stillness feels like a held breath.

I linger at the door, nerves flickering.
Through the walls I can hear a steady pulse
of chanting. I knock once, twice – nothing.
A ripple of uncertainty slides down my spine
as I slip round to the side of the house.

In the garden, I see them –
a gathering of women in a circle
a ritual of power unfolding.
They grip sticks as if holding the bones of the earth,
faces alive with fury and fire.
At the centre she stands, a storm given shape,
her voice commanding the wind itself to listen.

I dare not go any closer, yet I can't turn away.
I'm caught between breath and wonder.

Two hundred and sixty million Dalits in India.
The words tear through the air like arrows.
Four Dalit women raped . . .

The litany of violence echoes,
each number a heartbeat.
Two Dalits murdered,
two Dalit homes torched
every day
every day
every day.

The women rise as one, a tidal wave of anger
surging from their lips.
So what do we want? Her voice pounding like a war drum.

Justice! they roar, fists in the air
holding the sky in their fingers.

I am rooted to the spot, shaking, as if
struck by the electric current of their rage.
This woman, she is not real, not of this world.
She is flame and fury, a force that can't be undone.

At her feet, a tiger, its golden eyes gleaming,
unblinking, her silent guardian.

My skin prickles, heart pounding.
She is a goddess, and I'm no longer on the sidelines.

I've crossed the threshold.

Legend

Legend has it
that women with a thirst for revenge
come from these parts.

The Chambal River with its ancient curse
hunts for those who seek to revolt.
Women with rebellion in their blood.

She calls you to her, inviting you to sink
beneath her ancient currents, where she'll
whisper insurrections and stir storms within you.

Her waters flood your veins, carve through your soul,
turning you inside out, unmaking you,
until you rise, reborn, unbroken.

Shalini

This warrior, she doesn't wait for justice,
she carves it out with her own hands.
She trains an army of women and girls,
she fights fire with fire,
going after those who thought they could take
whatever they wanted, when they wanted.

The self-made gods run from her in fear.
They say she inspires change
in the deepest darkest corners,
lifting the fallen,
dragging down the self-made gods from their ivory towers,
leaving a trail of fear in them and hope for the rest of us.

They whisper she's Kali reborn,
goddess of destruction and rebirth,
feared and adored, with a tiger by her side,
a sword in her hand, cutting through the lies,
and slaying her enemies.

And when she leaves, she doesn't go alone,
she takes girls and women with her.
Those who were told they couldn't rise
flock to her, asking to join her army.
So, she takes them, and makes warriors of them,
so they need never live in fear again.

I have only seen her through a screen,
pictures on social media, stories in magazines
but to see her standing here in the flesh,
it's unreal.

Shalini looks up, her eyes lock with mine,
and for a moment, time ripples.

Have I gone back in time? she says.
You look just like her.
She smiles a knowing smile.
Welcome. I've been expecting you, Rizu.

First impressions

You've been expecting me?

News travels, she says.
I've heard whispers of you,
echoes of your mother,
old stories rising like ghosts.

She gestures for me to come closer.
I'm hesitant. *The tiger*, I say,
fear evident in my voice,
as he stands on all fours, staring.

His name is Rama, she says,
and he won't hurt you.

Rama, I repeat.
It's a beautiful name.

A silence lingers between us,
the weight of what I've come for looming heavy.
Why are you here?

It's at that moment I realize I don't even know.
I'm silent, feeling stupid for coming here.
What was I thinking?

I don't know, I finally admit.
My friend was . . . murdered.
The word lands like lead.
I realize it's the first time I've said it.

I don't usually help people like you.
*My work is for people who **really** need my help.*
Your people are dangerous for me.

*My people **are** your people,*
you grew up the same as me.

I feel her bristle,
reminded of a life she's tried to forget,
one she can't escape from.

My past bears no resemblance to my present.
I chose a life of service.

My friend, Jaya, is dead.
The people who did this can't get away with it.

Then why haven't you called the police?
They love helping the rich.

I have so much I want to say,
yet the words stick in my throat,
stuck, unable to escape.

I read about your troubles,
your story made it into the Kota Times.
She pauses, stroking Rama.
I understand what you've endured,
but the Jains are a powerful family . . .

But what about Jaya?
She was our housekeeper,
she wasn't rich, privileged . . .
I plead, my voice shaking.

To challenge the Jains would disrupt the ground beneath us.
They would ruin everything I have built with a mere flick of their wrist.
I try to help as many as I can, really, I do, but the Jains,
they can get out of anything. They know people in the highest of places.
To bring justice for this girl would mean taking down a very powerful family.
I'm sorry. You should go back home.
You are freer than most. Believe me.

But didn't you say once that we are not free until we are all free?
I heard you, on the TV.
I'm not free, Shalini.
I'm scared, Shalini.
I've lost everything.
Despite what you see and think, I'm not free.

Shalini

Old memories

Old memories stir,
like dust unsettled by the wind.
When betrayals resurface
it's hard not to punish the daughter
for the sins of the mother.

But, she's a girl,
a young woman in need, desperate.
This is what I do,
this is how I give,
this is how I serve.

She's seen horrors,
felt the cold grip of fear,
and she could be next.
She needs me.
This is why I'm here,
why they find me,
why I don't turn away.

I see it in her eyes,
the terror, the plea,
the same look
I've seen a hundred times.

But still . . .

When old betrayals resurface
like a stubborn wound
it's hard not to punish the daughter
for the sins of the mother.

A quiet spark

And yet,
this one is different,
a fire that flickers beneath the surface,
she stands, not apart from the others,
but glowing in a subtle, unmistakable way.
There's something . . .
But what?
I sense a quiet fire waiting to ignite.

The desire to turn her away is strong,
but there's a pull.
We both see it,
Rama and I.
I sense it in the way he stands,
his gaze unwavering,
his head ever so slightly leaning forward,
almost bowing in her presence,

both of us wondering what it means
to be drawn to brilliance
before it blooms.

Ultimatum

Call your mother, she says.
I walk behind her at pace
as she strides ahead of me
Rama by her side.

I don't want to,
she'll just tell me to come back.

Of course she will – she's your mother,
that's exactly what she's supposed to do.

She holds out a phone,
I don't reach for it.

I won't let you stay without her permission.
I said the Jains were dangerous for us –
the family your mother married into is no different.

My family are nothing like Sonu's.

Jaya, your housekeeper,
I'm guessing she's been disposed of?

Yes.

Without a trace?

Yes.

Exactly. You see what you're all capable of?
I don't want any trouble.
Call her.

She pushes the phone into my hand.

Sits.
Waits
and listens.

A difficult conversation

Rizu?
She knows it's me
before I speak.

Her voice quivers
like she's holding back tears.
Come home, she pleads,
please come home.

I tell her I can't.
I tell her I won't.
I tell her I'm staying.

She says she'll come get me,
drag me back.
You can't stay there!
Her voice hard.

We go round in circles
her desperation
my defiance
neither of us willing to give in.

But then her voice switches, softer now –
I need to talk to Shalini.
Please, Rizu, let me speak with her.

I hold out the phone.
She wants to talk to you, I say
handing the weight of it over.

Shalini

When past meets present

Tell her to come home.
Meena's voice is insistent.

I've told her she can only stay with your blessing.

*I don't know what to do,
she's not listening to me.*
Meena's voice sounds strained.
How much do you know? she asks.

I think I'm caught up with the whole story.

*I'd come and get her
but I can't leave Raaj, he's a changed man.*
Her voice breaks
no longer hiding her distress
as she sniffs and sobs down the phone.

She can stay here until things calm down,
my voice softening.

Thank you. Keep her safe, won't you.

Of course. I keep all my girls safe.

A grudge held for so long
like a knot
refusing to untie itself,
binding us to our past,
finally frays a little.

*Your voice hasn't changed,
you still sound like you did twenty years ago*,
I say, smiling.

*I wouldn't recognize yours if it wasn't for your TV interviews.
It sounds deeper. More assured than it used to.*

I laugh a little.
Well, I've been doing a lot of talking.

*Yes, I know.
I've seen.
I've heard.*

One of us had to.
It's a low blow,
but I can't help it.
A part of me still needs Meena Malhotra
to see what she missed out on,
who she could have been.

*Don't make me feel worse
than I already have all these years.*

I can't make you feel anything,
I say.

It's all in the past now,
she says like she's wanting to sweep
everything under the carpet,
just like before.

Is it? It came back to haunt you pretty quickly.

What do you want me to say?
I don't know what else to do, Lini.

My breath catches in my chest.
No one's called me that in years, Meena.

I still remember the old you.
I think I hear a smile in her voice.
Please look after my daughter.

We hang up,
hearts heavy, hands shaking.
I stare at this scared girl,
the daughter of a woman
I thought I'd never see or hear from again.
My past crashing into my present.

So, it looks like you're staying, I say.

Thank you, she says, over and over.
Tears she was too tired to release
come flooding out.

But if you're staying, I say,
you must make yourself useful.
You're part of a team here,
there's no room for preciousness,
no space for tantrums.
The electricity is fickle,
the water's not always warm,
but we make do.
You'll be cooking, cleaning,
no one gets waited on here.
We work together side by side.
I look at her.
Are you up to it?

Between fear and friendship

This home is beautiful, Shalini,
I say, eyes tracing the carved balcony,
its intricate patterns catching the fading light.

What did you expect? A mud hut?
she teases, her smile playful.

No, of course not,
I stammer, my cheeks flushing with heat.

In a tent in the ravines like a fugitive?

No . . . I just . . .

Don't worry, I'm just teasing.
She leads me into a room,
dorm-like, with beds at each corner.

You'll sleep here tonight,
the girls will make up a bed for you.
Meet Annika, Leela, Sampat and Phoolan.
Leela is my second in command,
she'll help you feel settled in,
she says, smiling, before shutting the door
and leaving us alone.

Hi, I say shyly,
their faces blurring, names fading,
my heart beating too fast.
All I feel is fear.

I'm apprehensive, unsteady,
wondering how to step forward
into this new, strange space.
These girls . . .
What will they think of me?
What will they see?
Will they be another
Sonu, Preeti, Mia and Tanya,
with cruel laughter and scathing words?

Annika clears a space for me,
rolling out blankets
and placing pillows with practised hands.

Ma will get you a bed soon,
but for now, this will have to do,
she says, her voice kind,
but I can't quite trust it yet.

It's fine, I murmur, sitting down,
though the floor feels cold and foreign.
I mean, it's perfect,
I lie, because I don't want to seem ungrateful,
though I've never slept on the floor in my life.

How long are you staying? Leela asks.

I fumble for an answer,
feeling exposed,
feeling judged.
How long?
A few days?
A few months?

I've been so caught up in running,
I never stopped to think.

I don't know,
I manage, my voice thinning,
uncertainty spilling out.

No rush, Phoolan says,
her voice soft,
you have time to decide,
permanent, or not.

Permanent?
The word settles heavily,
like a weight pressing down on my chest.

You'll see, Sampat adds.
Ma has a way of holding you,
drawing you in.
You come here thinking you'll leave,
but most of us don't.

Never return?
That thought hadn't even crossed my mind,
but the idea plants itself deep,
its roots twisting,
taking hold of my thoughts.

But now that it's there . . .

I lie down on the tiled floor,
the room spinning slowly around me,
the ceiling a canvas for my anxiety.

I take deep, deliberate breaths,
and for the first time in weeks,
my heartbeat slows,
and my mind begins to quiet.

I put my hand on my heart,
feeling its rhythm,
steady now, calm.

Maybe . . .
Just maybe . . .
I never return.

First steps

Annika glances at me, lips twitching,
trying not to laugh as I fumble,
all thumbs in a bowl of spices.
My fingers burn, a stinging under my nails,
and a tear sneaks down my cheek.
I reach up, instinctive.

No, Rizu, no.
She slaps my hand away, gentle but firm,
Don't wipe your eyes, or you'll be crying all day.
Have you never cut chillies before?

I stare at her, eyes watering.
She sighs, leaning in,
her fingers dancing through onions and garlic,
like she's known this rhythm since birth.
Onions, garlic, ginger, chilli.
Have you never made dhal?
She pauses, eyebrows arched.
Or a sabzi? A chapati?

I cough, embarrassed.

Have you ever made anything?

I put a pizza in the oven once.

A collective gasp of disbelief
echoes around the kitchen.

The other girls chuckle,
shaking their heads as if I've confessed
I've never seen the sun.

She laughs. *Wow.*
You people really do nothing for yourselves.

I smile, embarrassed,
but they pull me back in,
the teasing lightening the room,
as they guide me,
laughing and showing,
each move a lesson,
each laugh a tender nudge,
as I stumble through the kitchen,
learning step by step,
in this new world
of flavour and warmth.

Worlds apart

I no longer have the serums,
the make-up,
the clothes.

But still, I know how to wear a mask.
How to change my voice,
my movements,
how best to blend.

That's the way to be, right?
I don't know any other,
to blend is safety,
to blend is survival.

I watch the other girls,
study their stride,
how they stand,
how they wear their skin
in the world with such ease.

They seem so settled
so sure, so solid within themselves,
laughing as loud as they like,
speaking as strong as they please.

They talk of big dreams,
bold ideas,
how to fix what's broken,
how to fight,
how to rescue the lost.

I watch,
I wait,
I wish,
I learn,
in a bid to change.

I try to speak the same as them,
to stretch beyond myself,
to be better than my fears,
imagine a life I could touch,
a world I could shape.

But despite the disguise,
and practised gestures,
I'm still me.
Still shrinking,
still in hiding.

In a crowd, yet isolated,
voices swirl around me,
laughter dances on the edges,
always out of reach.

Words feel heavy on my tongue,
conversations slip through my fingers.
Their world seems so bright,
filled with ease and belonging.

My life was so different.
It's not that I miss it,
but I wonder how I'll ever fit in here.
Everything feels – unrecognizable.

I call home, seeking an echo of something familiar,
but even my mother's voice seems detached.
I miss her, of course,
but I sense a subtle distance growing between us.
I wonder, does she feel it too?

And my father?
I still don't know how to feel.
There are no words –
only silence brimming with everything left unsaid,
and I make no moves to heal what's broken.

I feel consumed by loneliness.
It's not just the girls,
it's the strangeness of everything.
I reach out, longing to bridge the gap
between this strange new place,
and the life I once knew
but my hand falters mid-air.

Being yourself

'Wherever you go, there you are.'

I thought leaving behind my old life,
Sonu and the gang,
would change me,
but here I am
still avoiding mirrors,
still wearing a mask.

Just let it go. Shalini looks at me,
her eyes soft with understanding.
I see how hard you're trying.
You won't find connection,
until you show them who you really are.

Who am I?
I've never known.

Her words linger,
a quiet challenge,
a hopeful nudge,
to uncover the person,
I'm yet to meet.

Rama's shadow

Rama trails behind me,
silent, powerful,
his gaze steady,
his presence calm.

Some of the girls watch from a distance,
whispers of fear in their eyes,
but I strangely feel none,
despite my own fear early on,
I feel only an unexpected calm.

His amber eyes flicker,
and something unspoken passes,
a quiet comfort
I can't quite explain.

From afar, Shalini watches,
her gaze thoughtful, maybe uneasy,
as her tiger, her protector,
now lingers close to me after only a short while.

I wonder if she worries,
about this curious connection.
I don't understand it myself,
all I know is, with him near,
I feel less alone.

A saviour

Each woman, each girl carries a tale.
Not all of them ran, not all had to bail.
Some Shalini saved, pulled from the fire,
some came searching, fuelled by desire.

I ran, says Annika, barely eighteen.
I came to Shalini last year.
I refused the advances of a man with power.
I reported him,
I'd had enough.
They accused me of being a witch,
tried to kill me.
I had no choice but to run.

I was married too young, says Phoolan, eyes alight.
When I fought to leave him
he spun lies with twisted tongues.

She saved me, Sampat's voice, so soft.
My neighbours accused me of causing their crops to fail.
It was just a smokescreen.
I reported my employers for abuse,
they wanted me gone. Shalini saved me,
before they came with a noose.

Leela was brave, Annika declares.
She stayed, she fought.
Even the witch doctor couldn't bring her down.

Not quite, says Leela, a few years older than us all.
Shalini got to me just in time.
Scooped me up when I couldn't see,
a bag of bones, broken and bruised,
she carried me away, I had no strength to refuse.
I owe her my life.

The stories spin on, a steady stream
of girls and women who dare to dream.

Shalini is the one who gathers the lost
pays the price no matter the cost.
They find their way, they seek her out
she gives them a home, a voice to shout.
A family, an education, with a stick in hand
they call her Ma, a new mother, she helps them stand.

They tell me their tales of battles won
of fights that blazed under the sun.
Always they speak of Shalini's fire
a goddess, a legend, one who inspires.
She tames tigers, and stands her ground
a true warrior woman, with a roar unbound.

Scrolling

In the dark, the screen glows,
fingers flick through endless posts,
faces frozen in perfect moments,
lives untouched, unchanged.

Sunny's smile twists my gut,
his lies still echo in my head.
He left me in pieces,
yet here I am,
needing to know his every move.

Sonu, Preeti, Mia and Tanya –
their laughter, their perfect pictures,
a world spinning on without me,
like I was never there.

I rage at how Sonu's life continues with ease,
her path unbroken,
while Jaya lies dead,
invisible, forgotten.

The hours blur,
each scroll digging deeper,
feeding the fire of my fury,
my obsession, my pain.

A hand reaches out,
Leela's voice breaks the spell.
Enough, she says softly,
You've been at this for hours, put it down.

She takes my phone,
and for a moment,
the world stops spinning.

My turn

They sit in a circle,
Phoolan, Sampat, Leela, Annika,
their faces softened, open,
they've shared their pain,
their stories,
now it's my turn.
But the words feel heavy,
every syllable a stone.

I cheated with my best friend's boyfriend,
I begin, voice barely a whisper.
The confession hangs in the air,
like a wound freshly opened.
I thought it was love,
now I realize it was just the idea of being wanted.

They don't look away,
their silence urging me on.
The accusations came next,
they called me a witch,
but Jaya, the only real friend I had,
Jaya was the one who paid the price.

Leela's brow furrows, not in judgement,
but in understanding the weight of what I carry.
It wasn't your fault, she says softly.

We heard of you before you got here,
Annika admits, *but we needed **your** truth,*
not the version in the news.
I agree Jaya deserves justice,
it makes my blood boil to hear what happened –

But Ma won't embroil herself with your kind, Leela interrupts.
It's too dangerous, too much money and power,
it could ruin everything she has built.

There's a pause. A shared breath between us.

Out there, she continues, *caste makes us strangers,*
the world doesn't belong to people like us,
it belongs to people like you.
Here, we're equals, but trust doesn't come easy.

I swallow the knot in my throat.
I get it, I murmur.
You thought I'd look down on you,
think I was better than you.
They look knowingly at each other,
and my face flushes with embarrassment.
I was afraid too – afraid of being pushed away.

The room seems smaller,
the space between us shrinking.
With Sonu and the gang,
it was always a contest.
Who was prettier, smarter,
who could fit in better.
Even with my best friends,
I never felt safe.

Leela's gaze softens.
We're not here to compete.
We work together,
girls come to us
and we give them a home,
help them belong.

Annika sidles up next to me.
So, you can relax,
nobody is out to get you.

I hear the words, soft and certain,
and I want to believe them
but trust is a muscle too worn from past betrayals.
Still, there is something different about these girls –
they are not in competition or calculating like the ones I once knew.

Annika sits beside me, close and comforting.
Rama creeps into our room and settles at my feet,
and somehow, without meaning to,
my shoulders ease, just a little.

A new bond

The room feels lighter,
walls that once divided us,
now start to disintegrate.

I never thought I'd find this, I say quietly.

Sampat smiles, a warmth in her eyes
that I hadn't seen before.
None of us did, but here we are,
strangers who have become something more.

The bond is still fragile,
new and delicate,
but real.

Shalini

Amends

I hope it's OK that I called? I wanted to check on Rizu.
Meena's voice, so small, still reserved.

Of course, you can call any time.
I try to soften but my words still have bite.
I tell her Rizu is fine
settling in, making friends, finding light.

So ... what's your life like in Delhi?
I ask, trying to make conversation.

I was a teacher for a while, she says.

And now ...

I gave it up, spent a decade on and off in bed.

Illness? My voice softer now.

I suppose, she says
but the weight in her words
pulls me in.

What was it? I press.

The past always finds a way of creeping up on you.
I couldn't stand to look at myself,
hiding what I did . . .
The more I tried to hold it down,
the deeper the cracks.
It got to the point, no matter how hard I tried,
I couldn't keep myself together.

I try searching for the right words
but I take too long,
long enough for Meena to ask,
Hello? You still there?

I consider all the things I could say,
the unsaid truths hanging in the air.
How could you stay silent?
How could you let them go free,
those girls with their guilt?
You let them get away with murder.
Together we could have got justice.
You let them ruin me –
my family, we had to move away.
Leave everything behind.
Do you ever say her name, Meena?
Gia, Gia, Gia.
Do you remember her?
And me –
you forgot me, until now,
when you need something from me.

But I stay silent.
I don't say any of that.
I don't need to –

I'm sure Meena hears it in the silence.
She can feel it in the empty space
between every word.

*We never would have worked,
you and me*, Meena finally says
like a confession.

I disagree, I say.
*We were two women
with fire in our hearts.
Meena –
we could have changed the world.*

*Your roar, Shalini,
it scared me.
I wanted change to spread like roots,
slow and steady, reaching deep.
You wanted to break the sky open
flatten the landscape
build from the dust.*

*That's not true, Meena.
I am a storm, I'll give you that.
But I never believed in destruction,
despite how I'm portrayed.
I do not **seek** violence,
but I understand when it's necessary.
Justice doesn't come without cost,
and sometimes
the world demands that we fight to preserve it.
I could always feel how my roar shook you,
but that fear?*

*That was your own shadow,
your own silence holding you back.
Don't blame my voice
for silencing yours.
You've always had a roar, Meena –
you just never let it rise.*

Peace

It's been a few weeks and
each morning, after our chores,
we sip sweet hot tea on the veranda.
Rama moves between Shalini and me
and together we look out,
watching the sun rise over the Chambal River,
its light dancing on the water.
It's so quiet here, so still, and the air smells fresh
unlike the smog that chokes New Delhi
or the endless roar of traffic that never sleeps.

My heart feels at home here.
Each morning a brand-new start –
feels like forgiveness
with air that smells like a second chance.
Each sunrise a rebirth
a day breaking open just for me
becoming someone I never knew I could be.

My old life of croissants and iced coffees
a fading memory, replaced with hot chai,
potato-filled parathas and the tang of home-made yoghurt.

I've even found a love for the work.
The scrubbing and sweeping, cooking and tidying.
I like using my hands, it feels good,
it gives me a sense of purpose –
a tiny cog in this family, helping it turn,
being part of something bigger than myself.

But every day, I wait.
I wait for Shalini to ask,
When are you leaving?
The thought of leaving terrifies me.
Home is where Jaya's ghost lingers
and where everything fell apart.

I don't want to go back.
I don't want to face the past.
There is something here,
something I need to find,
a reason, a truth,
a light to guide me through the darkness.

Disown

Ma's voice sounds weary.
When are you coming home?

I don't know, once I've figured out what to do.

When will that be? Her voice eager, hopeful.

I can't give you an exact date, Ma,
I'm still finding my feet,
trying to piece together the fragments.
I was told to come here, to fight –
I need to figure out what that means,
to find this so-called purpose.

You're missing so much school –

I'm done with school, Ma.
It's not compulsory for me to be there any more.

That's not the point – what about your future?
You're not thinking, Rizu!
She exhales slowly.
I miss you. The words tug at my heart.

I miss you too, Ma.
Every day.

Your father wants to speak to you.

No, Ma, please don't.

But, Rizu, he misses you –

I know, I'm sorry, but I can't,
I can't hear his voice,
without seeing her blood.

Sisterhood in motion

Phoolan kicks a stone across the yard,
her grin wide, daring.
Bet you can't hit that, she teases,
eyes sparkling with challenge.
I squint at the tin can,
unsure how to stand,
how to throw –

The stone flies wide.
Ha! You're terrible! Phoolan laughs,
but her voice is warm,
the kind of laughter that invites you to keep going.
I try again, this time with more aim, more intent.
I miss.

OK, OK, she says,
patting me on the back.
This time you'll get it.
I nod as she hands me a stone,
but before I have time to take my aim,
Sampat's voice cuts through the air,
a whirlwind of energy,
her hands flailing like a burst of light.

Hey, you two, I need you for my team!
She's already kicking the ball, her feet fast and free.
I drop the stone, turning to Phoolan.
Now this, I know I'm good at!
I was on the girls' football team at my school.

The ball skims across the earth, a blur of motion.
I sprint, eyes locked, focused.
Over here, Rizu! Sampat already in position,
ready for the pass.

Phoolan darts in, her energy electric.
Sampat, pass it quick! Her voice full of urgency and thrill.
Sampat smirks, a small flick of her foot
sends the ball towards Phoolan.

Go Phoolan! You've got this!
Annika yells from the other side, her enthusiasm bubbling over,
already moving, anticipating the next play.

Phoolan takes off, weaving through the girls,
her laughter ringing out like a challenge.
Catch me if you can!

Annika positions herself near the goal and raises her hand,
her voice cutting through the noise.
Phoolan, centre it! I'm open! she calls.

Phoolan grins, a quick kick of the ball,
sending it sailing towards Annika,
who controls it with ease, kicking it straight towards the goal.

We erupt in cheers as the ball hits the back of the net.
I run up, throwing my arms round Annika.
Nice shot!

Sampat jogs over, a satisfied smile on her face.
Teamwork! she says simply, her voice steady and proud.

Phoolan bounces on her toes, her energy undiminished.
Come on, let's keep going, she says eagerly.

I look at the girls and something stirs,
something quiet and warm.
I still don't know if I belong,
but for the first time,
I believe that I could.

Roots and wings

Leela is quiet,
but her presence fills the room.
She's sewing, hands quick and sure,
like she's been doing this forever.
I sit beside her, watching her needle move through fabric,
her fingers delicate and steady.

Need help? I ask,
not sure if I should.
I still feel a distance between us,
maybe because she's older,
wiser, carrying years I'm yet to touch.
Maybe I'm not ready
to meet her where she stands.
I feel small beside Leela,
like I'm still learning how to breathe.

She looks at me, and without a word
hands me a needle, a piece of cloth,
and the silent invitation to learn.

I fumble, the thread slipping through my fingers.
Leela doesn't rush, she just watches me,
then kindly shows me how to hold the needle,
how to guide the thread.

You didn't feel like football today? she asks.

No, I figured I shouldn't be spending so much time outside.
I've already gone, like, a million shades darker these past few weeks.

Leela puts down her sewing and looks at me with anger.
What did you just say?

Nothing. I mean . . . it's just . . .
I fight to find the right words.
I grew up with aunties who told me I was too dark,
like it was some kind of curse.
They told me to stay out of the sun!
I laugh, trying to hide the hurt I've uncovered.

She's looking at me now –
like she's unsure how to see me,
but there's something gentle in her eyes,
as if she feels for me.

Every shade of skin is beautiful, she says.
Colourism has no place here.
Her hand reaches for mine,
her grip warm and grounding.
Our dark skin is not a flaw.
She picks up a mirror.
I recoil, shaking my head.
She holds it out with a quiet insistence.
You need to see what I see, Rizu.
Reluctantly I glance.
You might see imperfection,
but I see something different:
strength, resilience,
a beauty far greater,
beyond skin-deep.

My fingers trace the contours of my face,
as if searching for flaws. I want to believe her,
but doubt has settled deep like an old scar.

I exhale, my breath shaky.
It isn't easy to let go of something that has lived inside me for so long.
But in this moment, I choose to hold her words close,
and let them settle in the spaces where doubt used to be.

Slowly, these girls begin to feel like the sisters I never had,
lifting me up in ways I never knew I needed.
Friendships built on trust with bonds growing stronger,
they start to reshape me.

A lesson

A trip into town sees me buying
a Bollywood movie.
Ma doesn't let us watch those.
Phoolan's words carry a warning
I choose to ignore.

In the evening we gather round a screen,
popcorn, crisps in hand,
watching Bollywood reveal its stories
of love, loss and revenge.

This one's a classic.
A mother cries for her son,
lighting candles, incense,
singing a song of sorrow,
and as if her heart can sense him,
he arrives, wind in his hair,
flying in on a helicopter.
Tears fall, mother and son reunited . . .

Rama walks over and sits by my side,
gently resting his head against my arm.
Shalini watches, her face stern.
She strides over to the TV and switches it off.
I don't think so, she says. *Not in this house.*

But it's just a bit of fun, I say, laughing.

Fun? For you, maybe.
These are films for the upper castes.
The so-called 'perfect caste'.

The hero, the heroine, the pure ones –
light-skinned and flawless –
their world revolves around caste and colour.
She looks at my face,
a map of confusion.
It's not always obvious, Rizu, but it's there,
hidden, in the subtext.
Bad boys and girls –
dark-skinned and lower caste –
get their comeuppance, never changing.
While the good remain godly, dancing, singing.
What if, she asks,
these girls could see themselves as teachers,
lawyers, politicians, leaders
with hopes, dreams, multidimensional lives with
aspirations and stories to tell?
These films keep our girls down,
keep them dreaming small or not at all.
We must be careful with the messages we consume,
the shows we watch, the adverts we take in,
the literature we read, the social-media influencers we follow.
These films tell them they are not good enough.
That is why they are not allowed in this house.
Stories shape our world, Rizu –
not just in Bollywood, but everywhere.

I thought it was harmless –
a bit of home, a fleeting comfort.
Guilt rises in my chest.
The truth behind Shalini's words settling in.

Thirst

Despite the sisterhood
the warmth of this new tribe
a thirst stirs deep within me –
I yearn for revenge.

Each day I take my phone
and I scroll through Sonu's life.
Her perfect untouched world
flashing across my screen.
Her laughter as if nothing broke.

She has a new boyfriend now
a fresh circle of admirers
still the queen of every party
still the most popular girl in school.

My bitterness grows, festers
like a seed watered by rage
and I feel it swell inside me.

Everything for them has got better
while my life has been torn apart.
My mother talks about selling our home,
starting again somewhere new.
My father, a ghost who sleeps through the days.
Sonu gets to carry on,
whereas my family are forced to scrub out their past,
looking for something new and clean
away from the wreckage of what was.

I can't shake the injustice of it.
It claws at my insides.
It's unfair,
it's not right.
I want to go back,
to return to that world to face her.
I want to fight.

A restless energy burns through me
and the desire for revenge
is a thirst that won't be quenched.

Visions

At night I sink into
a warrior-wandering dreamland.

I descend into a vivid dreamscape
where I am the goddess incarnate.

I dream of breathing fire, turning villages to ash,
unleashing my divine Shakti against forces of evil.

I wield my sword, slaying the self-made gods
and the tribes that follow them, my tiger by my side.

The men, the upper castes, they bow at my feet
while I break the chains of the oppressed.

When I wake I swear I can feel the heat of the flames
and the cold metal of the blade in my hand.

Shalini

Perception

I was told I had a sharp tongue.
I sliced my way through life.
I knew my rights.
I spoke the truth.
I dreamed of better.
I fought for more.
There is a misconception –
people in the West,
huh –
no, not even the West,
people here,
the city folk
in their fancy jobs
in glass towers,
the Bombay-ites,
Delhi darlings
they think . . .
village women don't know better,
don't want better.
They say,
They are happy as they are,
they wouldn't know how to dream,
they haven't seen how life could be,
they accept,
they retreat.
To those people I would like to say,
Do you not think they have eyes, ears, a brain?
You really think that they are happy to accept their fate?
This fate that would have them live a life of being perpetually oppressed.

It is the lie they tell themselves to make themselves feel better.
These women are not happy in their situation,
hell,
most are just resigned to it
because the chance to escape has not presented itself.
But it will.
Oh, Rizu, it will.

In awe

When she talks
I feel alive.
I feel capable of anything.
I feel like I could shake
the stars from the sky.

When she talks
I feel a fire ignite inside me
sparks travelling under my skin
a burning desire
to fiercely fight.

Shalini doesn't break my gaze
and I believe if I look close enough
I can see the light in her eyes
flickering
burning
the desire
the heat
pouring

                out.

When? I ask nervously.
Desperate to know when things might change.

I don't know but I'm putting my hopes on you, Rizu.

Me?
Why   me?

Why not   you?

I shuffle nervously.
I'm nobody.

Everybody is a somebody.
You're still here, you haven't left yet,
you'll see it soon enough.

See what? I'm sick of –

Sick of what?

Being told I'll see what's inside me.
That I'm born of fire.
What if it's all crap?
What if none of it is true?
What if I'm not special?

I feel guilty for everything.
Being here, living and breathing
when Jaya is not.
She didn't even get a proper funeral,
instead lying rotting in a quarry.
When I think about it,
it makes me want to rip my skin off.

She holds me to her as I cry.
It's OK. She strokes my hair. *It's OK.*
I don't mean to put pressure on you.
I just, I see it, that's all –
I see something special.

I make a promise to myself
that I'm going to make it right,
Jaya's death will not go unpunished,
those who started this should and will pay.

Decision time

So, tell me, she says,
you've been here long enough
to see how things work.
Are you staying or going?

I want to stay, but on one condition,
I say cautiously.

Shalini looks shocked.
I don't think the girls
have ever challenged her.

What? Her eyes wide.

You help me get justice, for Jaya.

OK, she says after a pause.
OK, I'll see what I can do.

I'm irritated.
Why isn't it an easy
'yes'
a heartfelt
'yes'
a firm, fierce
'yes'?

Why do you have to think about it?
I ask. Trying not to sound too abrupt.

Because your case isn't so easy, Rizu.
Your friend, Sonu Jain –

Yes, I know, she's from a very powerful family –

Well, if you know, her voice cutting now,
then you know how dangerous they are.
So, if you don't mind, I will have to think about it.

My breath feels heavy in my chest,
my eyes sting with disappointment.

Right, she says, picking up a stick
and throwing it to me.
You ready for your first lesson?

Lesson one

She takes a swipe.
It lands on my arm,
I scream out in pain.
Learn to block, she says.

She takes another swipe,
I stumble.
Learn to stand your ground, she says.

She takes another swipe,
I fall.
Learn to get up, she says.

Failing

I push myself every single day,
driven, determined for the fight ahead.
I thought this would be easy –
fighting would flow like breath.
I was an athlete at school,
always strong, always the champion.

But here, I stumble,
weakness spills from my muscles,
humiliation clings to every fall.

A hundred times I crash,
a hundred more I rise,
teeth gritted, heart pounding,
withholding a storm of blows.

My body is small,
not built for fight
but built for flight.

I'm used to running not holding my own.
I'm used to talking tough, but this is raw.
It's blood, sweat, muscle and tears.

Friends in arms

Annika, Phoolan, Leela and Sampat
coach me in their own time,
so when it comes to group practice
I'm not so behind.

Come on, princess!
What's the matter, break a nail?
Annika's laughter rings between blows,
a gentle sting to ignite my fire.
Careful, your tiara might slip.

You gonna cry or fight back?
Phoolan's eyes blaze, challenging me.
Sampat's voice cuts through –
Show us that silver spoon's worth something!

Leela's strength is constant and calming.
Enough running, time to stand your ground.

Their teasing fuels my fury,
turns frustration into grit.
Each strike, each fall,
a lesson etched in bruises and sweat.

Their laughter is kind,
a shield against the sting of defeat.
They lift me when I falter,
turning bruises into badges of honour.

Each fall, a lesson learned,
each rise, a testament to courage.
Together we forge a bond,
sisters in struggle, warriors in spirit.

Annika's fierce gaze burns,
Phoolan's steady hand guides,
Sampat's voice, a battle cry,
Leela's strength, my pillar.

We fight as one,
each strike more precise,
each move more fluid.
In their company
I find my place,
as a fighter reborn.

A beastly bond

Rama nuzzles at my calves,
a warmth I never thought I'd know.
At first wary of his untamed grace
now his presence soothes.

He sleeps at my feet,
his weight an anchor in the night,
a silent promise, a steady heart,
my beastly guardian in the dark.

He follows me through the day,
pacing beside me as I work,
a hunter's stride, yet softened –
and though his strength could break me.
I feel no threat, only trust.

A strange, surprising thing has happened.
Rama, a king, yet now he bends his head to me
as my protector, my shield.
Both of us roar with what we know to be true –
his strength is mine and in his wild company,
I'm mighty too.

Calling home

The phone trembles in my hand,
my mother's voice, soft and weathered.
Rizu, your father's here,
he'd love to speak to you.

My heart clenches a storm within.
I can't, Ma, don't ask me to.

Please, it might help him –
he's a changed man, Rizu.
Don't you miss him at all?

Echoes of Jaya's tears,
the weight of his choice,
all for me, for love,
but the cost too great to bear.

I choke back tears.
Of course I do, Ma.

Rizu, he's broken. He regrets it every day.
Ma's voice wavers, I feel the ache,
the pull of compassion, yet the wound still festers,
a chasm I can't cross.

I know he did it for me,
I know he suffers, but I can't, Ma,
I just can't.

It wasn't easy for me either,
she says after a long pause.
I couldn't stand to look at him.

Silence stretches,
a fragile thread between us.
How can you stay with him, Ma?

I knew the day you left I'd lost you,
I couldn't bear to lose him too.
Ma sighs, a sound heavy with heartache.
He's a good man who did a bad thing.
If you could see him, Rizu . . .
if you could just talk to him . . .
you'd see how broken, how disgusted,
how sorry he really is.

There's a war within my heart,
compassion and pain,
love and betrayal.
I know he's broken,
I know the weight he carries
but the past looms too large,
too raw, too real.

Maybe one day, Ma,
but not today.

He'll be waiting for you, Rizu,
waiting for the day you can forgive.

The line goes quiet,
but the echo lingers.

Battle cry

Some of these girls fly through the air
they are so lithe, so strong, so swift.

I feel clunky in comparison.
They teach me how to stand
how to strike, how to duck.

I fall and rise

    fall and rise

        fall and rise.

You have it in you, Shalini tells me.
Greatness is yours, but you have to believe it first.
No one else can do it for you.

We shout and fight.
We laugh and chant.
We fall and bleed
and build friendships
in the bonds of battle.

Changing

I used to speak in an affected drawl.
A mix of English and Hindi.
A voice that came from shallow breath,
all croaky and weak like they do on TV,
a voice shaped by the world I came from.

Now my words flow differently.
I let my mother tongue
dance off my lips
rolling in ways that feel real,
raw, ancient and powerful.

I've shed the skin of Western attire
and wrap myself in colours, in textures, in history.
The sari drapes over me like a second skin,
so light, so freeing, like shedding the layers of a life
I didn't even realize were suffocating me,
woven with stories I'm just beginning to understand.

I moulded myself into the girl
I thought I was supposed to be,
polished, shiny, unblemished.
Now I walk with these women,
this tribe of outcasts,
who've embraced the broken,
the beautiful flaws that make us whole.
They laugh without apology,
fight with fierce joy
and bleed like warriors.

And something inside me stirs,
something wild, untamed and deeply true.

I don't miss that old life.
I don't miss the false perfection,
the mask I used to wear.
Here, among these women
who have lost everything,
I am finding myself.

Losing sleep

I lie awake, staring into darkness,
my mind restless.
The echo of my mother's voice from earlier
weighs heavy on my heart.

When she spoke, I sensed something broken beneath,
a kind of silence masking a deeper ache.
Fear presses in with each breath.
With my father now in pieces,
who is there to hold her?

Annika turns beside me,
Rizu, you're keeping me awake with your tossing and turning.
She sits up. *What's wrong?*

My ma, I whisper, looking at her through the dark.
She needs me, but I don't know if I can go back.

Afraid of what will happen? she asks.
I nod, but it's more than that.
*I'm scared of what I'll see when I look at her,
what she'll ask of me.*
Tears build behind my eyes.
I'm not sure I have it in me to do what she'll want.

*You can't let fear dictate your actions.
You are stronger than you give yourself credit for, Rizu.
You already did the hardest thing – you left,
made a life for yourself here.
No one can force you to do anything you don't want to do.*

No matter what your ma might ask of you,
you have it in you to walk your own path.

Annika's words hover in the quiet
but they don't quite land.
Leaving was hard, but going back?
I'm too scared of what I'll find.
I close my eyes but the image of my parents,
their faces worn by time and regret, won't leave me.

What if Ma's not OK?
She's had to deal with everything all alone.
The thought paralyses me, and in the dark
the burden of the decision pushes harder.

Rama rests his head on my feet,
but his comfort doesn't feel like enough.
I shuffle away from him, heart pounding.
The truth is, it's not just about me –
I have to know she's all right,
and I have to face my father.

Home

I sit between them,
my father and mother,
and the room feels like it's holding its breath.
Ma's hands are trembling, while Papa sits, eyes cast down,
shoulders shaking with silent sobs.

Ma talks, her words breaking like glass.
I saw it coming, Rizu, I felt it the first time you called.
You slipped away from me the second you met Shalini.
But here at home, the chaos still rages on.
Jaya's family have come asking, hungry for answers.
I feel sick.
I think of her all the time.
Ma chokes on her words.
It's a never-ending nightmare, Rizu.
I see that night so clearly,
I think of every moment,
I go over it and over it.
What could we have done differently?
We could have saved her . . .

So what now? I whisper, holding her close,
fearing if I let go, she'll shatter.

Whenever they came round, we hid,
but we couldn't keep that up for long.
So, we told them we don't know.
She must have run away.
I wanted to tell her,
when I looked into her mother's eyes,
I wanted so badly to tell her.

The woman was beside herself.
But to tell would mean prison.
We'd lose everything.

Papa doesn't move,
his hands twisted in his lap.
He doesn't even bother wiping his tears.
I watch as his chest heaves,
each breath a struggle.

The hysteria might have subsided, Ma continues,
no more fits or faints, but I'm branded, outcast,
the city's whispered curse.
It's probably best you're not here, Rizu,
it wouldn't be safe.
But when we move,
somewhere new, somewhere safe,
promise me you'll return?

I look at her, knowing
I couldn't possibly promise such a thing.
Instead I nod, and hold her,
trying my best to soothe the pain.

We can heal, be a family like before.
Your father can start a new business,
I'll go back to teaching –
how does that sound?

Her words hang heavy,
hope woven into every plea,
but I can't find my voice.
She reaches forward,

cupping my face with her hand.
We'll be whole again soon, I swear it, Rizu.

I stay silent for what feels like forever,
then the words tear from me:
Even if you move, Ma,
I can't come and live with you again.

Her eyes widen, her breath catches.

I don't see how it could ever work.
I'm not the girl who left
and I can't live with Papa, not after –

I glance at Papa, feeling the ache of all the things unsaid.
His shoulders shake, but still, he doesn't speak.
He stands, and when he moves, it's like his body betrays him.
He's slow, unsteady and stumbles towards me,
kneeling on the ground. His hand reaches out,
touching my feet, asking for forgiveness.
I flinch. I want to pull away, but I don't.

Please, Rizu, please forgive me.
I hate myself for what I did,
but I did it to save you –

That's not how I wanted saving.
I can't bear that her life was taken for mine.
I stand, needing space from them both.
Staying with Shalini,
it's the only way I can make any of this right.
If that's even possible.

What about your education, Rizu?
Your future?

Honestly, I feel like I'm learning more from Shalini
than I ever would at school. The world she's opened up to me,
I've never felt so alive. She's taught me to see beyond
everything I thought was important, to think for myself, to be truly free.

Their tears fall like rain
and I stand in the downpour
knowing I've already gone
from here
from them
from the girl I used to be.

The enemy

As I leave, she arrives.
We stand on either side of the gate,
divided by iron
and everything that's passed –
betrayal, deceit.

Her eyes widen in shock
then shrink in fear.
She sizes me up
scanning every change –
rougher, rawer, no more gloss.
Stronger. Simpler.
No designer labels, no fragile frame,
skin darker from the sun, no make-up.
Just me, stripped down to the bones.

You've changed, she stutters.

You haven't, I reply,
words cutting through the air.

Where have you been? she asks.

Nowhere. Everywhere.
The truth wrapped in riddles.

What does that even mean?

She doesn't understand,
not yet, but she will.

When you least expect it, Sonu,
your perfect little life will collapse.

Her eyes flash with defiance.
You don't scare me.

You should be scared, Sonu.
You should be terrified of me.
I reach through the bars,
grab her wrist, she screams.
You will pay, Sonu.
You will pay for what you did.

She struggles to pull away,
I pull in, closer,
rage like fire beneath my skin.
I've pictured this moment,
every sleepless night,
rehearsed what I'd say,
how I'd make her feel,
what I'd feel.

But standing here now,
there are no rehearsed words,
only the raw roar of everything inside me,
all the pain, the regret, the fury,
bursting free in a scream.

Sonu

The victim

We meet at the gate,
the lies I told,
the guilt and shame of it all
comes rushing over me.

She stares, her eyes hard as stone
and I'm frozen, fear curling inside.
She looks different, rougher, stronger,
like she's shed her old skin.
I feel so small.
Guilt gnaws at me through the bars.

You've changed, I manage,
trying to sound more confident than I feel.
Her reply slices through the air.
Her eyes burn into me
as she threatens me
telling me my life will fall apart
when I least expect it.

A chill runs through me.
I try to stand tall,
try to fight the fear rising in my chest.
You don't scare me, I say, but even I hear the lie.

Suddenly her hand shoots through the bars
grabbing my arm, her grip like steel.
I scream, the sound bursting from me.
Her words slam into me,
the weight of my shame crashing down
along with a tidal wave of guilt that I've been drowning in.

Every day a lie
self-hate rising
knowing I don't deserve to be standing here.
I don't deserve to be alive.
She pulls me closer
I feel her shaking
but I can't fight back.
I'm already shattered inside
pieces of me barely holding on.

Every night since it happened
I've been haunted
waking up gasping for breath
choking on the memory of what I did
what I started.
I've imagined this moment
her rage, her revenge
and now here it is
and I have no strength left to resist.

She screams.
A roar from deep within.
It's the sound of everything
I've been hiding from.

Progress

We gather in a circle
the firelight flickering in our eyes.
Shalini stands tall in the centre
her stick raised high above her head.
This is our weapon, she declares,
our shield against those that seek to crush us.
This is how we fight
this is how we win
this is how we survive.
Are you with me?

Every session starts the same.
We all respond in unison,
voices rising –
We are with you!

Louder, Shalini demands.

We are with you!

I can't hear you.

WE ARE WITH YOU!

She looks directly at me, calling me forward.
You've been here for months, Rizu.
There is strength and skill there,
but you still have a lot to learn.
Pick up your stick.

I hesitate for a moment,
feeling the weight of the circle's eyes on me.
My legs tremble slightly.
Strike me, she says. Her voice firm but teasing.
Go on. Don't be scared. You can't hurt me.

I raise the stick, my grip uncertain, and swing.
Shalini blocks it with a swift, practised motion.
Again, she commands.
I strike once more, harder this time,
but again, she parries with ease.
Each attempt seems futile
yet with every clash of wood
Rama roars softly, circling us, closer,
his eyes on Shalini
as if he senses my frustration.

He stalks the edge of the circle
his gaze never leaving the fight.
Whenever Shalini strikes me down
I see the tension in his muscles
as if he might leap to my defence.
A look of concern sweeps across Shalini's eyes.

Step aside, she orders.
She calls Leela up to demonstrate.
They clash with ferocity
like two warriors from mythic battle.
Watch closely, Rizu, Shalini shouts.
Do you see how it's done?

I'm back in the centre,
a slight tremor in my hands,
but something is changing inside me,
growing stronger with each breath.
I lunge, I strike, a little hesitation at first
but faster now, more controlled.
Shalini's army watches,
and though my legs feel weak,
I push through,
the trembling starting to fade,
replaced by a sense of purpose,
quiet but sure.

Renewed determination

Weeks pass in a blur,
sweat staining my skin,
bruises blooming like dark flowers.
I train harder,
becoming something else,
someone else.
Not the girl I was
but the woman I need to be.

I fight like a goddess now,
like Kali on her lion,
her sword raised high,
moving with the grace and fury of a storm.
I lunge, I duck,
I soar through the air
becoming a blur of speed and strength.
Faster,
stronger,
fiercer with every breath.

With every strike
I see Sonu's face,
haunting and bold.
With every step
injustice echoes in my bones.
Every fall ignites the fire inside me.

Even Rama, once only at Shalini's side,
sits by my side, eats from my hand,
his massive form curled protectively at my feet.
Has his loyalty drifted?
Has he chosen me?
Shalini seems rattled.
I sense she feels it,
her eyes wary when Rama pads over to sit near me,
his golden eyes watching her as I rise to fight.

I feel the fire that runs through my blood.
Jhano, my ancestor, born of flame,
her strength is part of me.
I sense her in every movement,
her spirit igniting something deep inside me.

I notice something in Rama's eyes too,
a trust, a recognition of sorts.
He knows who I'm becoming.
He sees the light I carry within
and the power waiting to break free.

I am no longer the girl I was.
And the tiger knows it.

Shalini

The goddess and the beast

Rama, raw and regal,
his amber eyes aglow with ancient allure,
I see him, drawn to Rizu, magnetic and fierce,
her spirit wild, a storm surging beneath calm skies.

Does he feel her fire, her fierce connection,
or is it the pulse of her past that pulls him from me?

Tigers – tales of terror and triumph,
guardians of the gods, fierce in their grace,
their roar a hymn, their stride a prayer.
Is it the goddess in her blood that now holds his gaze?

I watch him change, his path now veering,
his loyalty, once mine, begins to sway,
his steps now aligning with her destiny,
a bond breaking, threads of trust disintegrating.

The shift stings, a reminder
of allegiances lost, of loyalty gone.
In the quiet I'm left to question
what this change, this loss, might bring.

First taste of revenge

It takes two hours to get there by bus.
We're thirty strong and fill every inch.
The bus stops, picking up strangers who gasp, eyes wide,
at Rama, sleeping in the aisle,
his sleek body stretched in calm menace.

He won't hurt you, I promise. It's perfectly safe.
I've raised him since he was a cub, Shalini states.
Some sit but at a distance
while others wait for the next bus.

Her confidence is a force of nature,
bold and unapologetic.
Bringing a tiger on to a bus is nothing to her.
She stands cool as ever, while passengers shrink back.
No one dares question her,
not when she has a tiger at her command.

Why don't we hire a vehicle? I ask.
It would be much quicker.

Shalini's smile is sharp, her words a blade.
Oh really? I hadn't thought of that,
she says sarcastically.
Travelling by public transport
serves a purpose: we must be seen,
felt, rippling through the country,
a wave of fear and strength.
Every girl, every woman on this bus
must see us, know we are here,
a fierce promise in flesh.

I watch as she delivers speeches on the bus,
her voice rising like a banner
letting other passengers know who we are.
We want justice! we chant, fists high.
It's electric – I feel myself
clutching at my stick,
ready for battle.
She tells everyone where we go,
what fight we face.

Today's war is for Jacintha,
a young woman, ravaged, wronged,
her family hunted by lies.
Her rapist calls her a witch,
twists her pain into a spell she never cast.

Wherever Shalini goes, the press always seems to follow.
It makes things intimidating, keeps the police officers on edge –
it's hard to be complacent when cameras are in your face.

Most of us gather outside the police station,
but a few of us manage to squeeze inside.
I can barely contain my excitement watching her work.

Shalini handles the press and photographers with ease,
her voice commanding attention.
And then there's Rama – his massive body rising beside her,
paws thudding heavily on the desk.
His threatening snarl a rumbling storm.
The officer gulps air, chokes on his spit.

We're filing charges, Shalini declares.
Why is that man not in prison?
Why does her family suffer while he roams free?

B-b-black magic, he stammers.
They say she's a w-w-witch.

W-w-witch, Shalini mocks.
We all know why they are saying that.
Men like him think girls like her are their property,
theirs to prey on whenever they wish.

Rama's deep, thundering roar
has the room drenched in fear.

I think we should go to this house
and make an arrest, don't you?
The officer nods, pale, frozen.

The tension in the room is electric,
and I can't look away.
Rama's presence, Shalini's power –
it's a force that makes the world stop and listen.

We march. An army of fury,
our sticks beat the ground like drums.
Justice for Jacintha, we chant,
a cry that fills the streets.
Doors open, faces watch,
little girls stare in awe.
Some join, tiny fists raised,
echoes of fighters yet to come.

A young girl grabs my hand
her eyes bright with pride.
I want a stick, she says.

You can have one, I reply, and give her mine to hold.
How does that feel? I ask.
Good, she says, and continues to march by my side,
a warrior born in an instant.

After the arrests, we meet Jacintha's family.
Grateful words, tears of hope,
but Shalini is firm.
If he walks free, we'll be back.

She speaks softly with Jacintha,
asks if she's safe, if she'll stay.
I want to come with you, she says.
An accusation of witchcraft doesn't wash away.
It stains forever.
If I stay, my family are still in danger.

Then it's settled. Shalini smiles.
You're one of us now.

On the ride home, I watch Jacintha,
newly born into our fold,
helpless now, but soon,
soon she'll be a warrior.
I think of the girl who held my hand,
beating the earth with my stick.
Shalini saves, yes,
but she also ignites,
a fire that spreads,
that turns fear into power
and women into flames.

A second taste

We travel all day,
arrive under the cover of night,
the atmosphere steeped in tension,
shouts and screams leading us to the heart of the village.

An old woman, alone, cowers inside her home,
accused, abandoned. Another witch, they say.
Her crime? Living too long, living alone.

Shalini strides forward, Rama growls,
a rumbling sound that carves through the mob,
parting them like water.
I grip my stick, my pulse surges –
finally, *finally*,
this is what we trained for,
this is where I let loose.

But before I can take a swing,
Shalini's hand clamps round my wrist.
What are you doing?
Her eyes burning into mine.
You take action on my command.
I bristle with anger.
I look at my comrades.
Annika shakes her head,
a warning, for me to keep quiet
and Leela takes my hand,
to help calm me.

Rama circles, holding the mob in place
while Shalini calls the police.
Once again we stand, sticks in hand
tapping the ground, chanting,
a rhythm that vibrates the night air.
It feels powerful but I can't help thinking,
Why not use our force?
Why not crush them, show them our strength?

When the crowd breaks,
the old woman lets us in,
her eyes wet with tears.
What did I do to deserve this?
A six-year-old accusing now.
'Didi Sharma put a curse on me.'
Right outside the gates of the school.
I brought up that girl.
I've brought up so many of the children.
I even bathed and changed her mother when she was a child.

Will you leave with us? Shalini asks.
It's the only way you can save yourself.

But the woman's eyes are tired
her body heavy with bruises.
Let God have his plan.
I'm done running.
It never ends for people like me . . .

Back at home the fire inside me boils over.
I confront Shalini.
What's the point of the sticks?
All this training just for us to chant?

Don't you want blood?
Why are we holding back?

Her voice is calm, but firm.
Rizu, she says, *the sticks are for self-defence, not revenge.*
Justice isn't an eye for an eye. It's through words,
through education. The sticks protect us if they ever try to strike.
I rarely use violence, despite what they say about me in the media.
True change isn't born from blood.
There is no point tearing something down, Rizu,
if you're not ready to build something beautiful in its place.
She places her hands on my shoulders.
I can tell you're still frustrated, Rizu.
I know you are still aching for justice for Jaya,
but you must practise patience – this is how we do things around here.

Her words cut deep,
like a dull blade running through me.
I search her face, waiting for more –
but all I see is restraint.

I understand now why she's taking her time
to decide about the Jains.
She doesn't have what it takes.
My belief in her,
the warrior I thought she was,
begins to fray at the edges.
My hands curl into fists,
itching for more than just talk.

I didn't come here to watch and wait.
I came to fight.

The third

Anger mounts as protesters flood the street.
A murder, a young woman, a life cut short.

And there she is, Shalini,
in front of the cameras,
cool and calm, standing with poise,
slicing through the noise.
Justice, crime, prison,
arrests, innocence, protests.

She shines, commands attention
but all I see is – talk, talk, talk.

I grip my stick, feel the tension
coil dangerously inside me.
I've been quiet for long enough –
I grab the girls and take them to one side.
We train every day, I say, *we've all learned to fight,*
but all she does is speak while the world burns.

Phoolan's face is torn, thinking.
Leela shakes her head.
This is her way, she whispers.
Sampat hisses, *Shush!*
You can't say things like that, Rizu.
Annika nods, then shrugs.
What can we do?

Exactly.
What. Can. We. Do?

An announcement

We are all brought together,
sitting in the central room of the house.
Moments like this are reserved for big announcements.

Shalini perches in front of us,
she takes a deliberate deep breath.
I have decided to stand for election.

The room jolts with a collective gasp.
Then erupts into uneasy murmurs,
Who?
    When?
        How?
            What does this really mean?

She holds up her hand.
I know, you all have questions,
and I'll do my best to answer them.

But I slice through the polite chaos.
Why?
My voice cold, unyielding.

Shalini's eyes flicker, caught off guard.
I thought your fight was grassroots.
I drive my words like daggers.
If you're elected, how will you maintain that connection?

She looks at me, her smile forced.
If anything, Rizu, she says, her tone too smooth,
I'll wield even greater influence.
I'll help countless more at grassroots,
not just with temporary patches,
but real, lasting change.

I watch her closely,
but all I feel is the widening chasm.
Her words sound like promises,
but her eyes, they whisper something else.

My turn

When will we go back to my home? I ask.
Months have passed,
surely it's my turn now.

Shalini takes a deep breath,
sits me down with a gaze that burns.
What I'm about to say might upset you.

My heart thrums, beating wild.
I can't go back to your home, Rizu.
I've made my decision.
I'm sorry, I know it's not what you were hoping for.

Her words hit like a blow.
What's done is done, Rizu.
But here, if you stay,
you can make a real difference.
So many girls, lost and forgotten,
need you. You should see that as justice for Jaya.
I've seen you change, Rizu, and
it's been beautiful to witness
the warrior you've become.

She sees my face harden.
I know you're upset,
but look around – ripples are spreading.
Maybe it's time to let go of what happened to you.
Your work here is so much more than that.

And that's it.
Just like that, it's over.
My home, my family,
justice for Jaya,
denied,
rejected.

I pace my room.
The walls closing in,
my friends watching,
their voices soft,
trying to calm me.

She's been stringing me along all this time,
and for what? She was never going to help.
Saying she won't because she's scared of the rich,
yet here she is, starting a campaign to get into government –
she's a hypocrite!

Shalini has a point, Sampat says.
She never deals with city people.

I don't want to hear it! I shout.
She doesn't do any of this to really help.
She's in it for the attention.
She loves it! Don't you see how she lights up
when the cameras are around?
It's not a coincidence when the press shows up
everywhere we go either. She calls them, it's all planned.

So what if it is, Leela says, her eyes holding something deeper –
something that tells me she knows more than she's letting on.
It helps spread awareness, so we can seek real change.
I'm sorry you're not getting the justice you want,
but her fight is here, in the villages,
with women and girls who have no voice.

The fact I come from money
doesn't mean I have a voice! I scream.

Home truths

Rizu, you speak of justice –
Leela's words are biting, her voice like fire –
but you know nothing.
You've lived within walls of marble,
with gold in your eyes.
Her gaze is hard, cold,
like she can see right through me.
She gestures around the room,
taking in Phoolan, Sampat, Annika.
But you know nothing of hunger,
where every day is a fight,
where tomorrow's just a prayer.
You think your pain, your loss,
is the only one that matters?
You want justice for Jaya?
Then stop seeing her death as a tragedy
that doesn't have your blood on it.

Her words land where my breath should be,
landing with such force they bruise the air inside.

Take it easy, Leela. Phoolan's voice is soft.

No, I've had enough.
She's behaving like a spoilt little rich bitch.
See the bigger picture here, Rizu.
Shalini has a vision and it's
greater than the sum of us all.

I thought the same, in the beginning,
but now I'm not so sure.

My chest tightens as I speak.
There's a word for people like her – fame-seeker.
She spends most of her days doing interviews –

She has a message to spread, Leela interrupts.

My mind reels, anger rising like a tsunami.
She has her own agenda –
sometimes I think glory is her motivation.

That's not true.
Leela and I come face-to-face.
You've only been here a short while,
you know nothing of the lives she's saved,
the lives she's changed. Her methods might not be perfect,
but they are hers and they work.

I look to the other three,
their faces unreadable.

She talks of ripples of change, I say,
but we are in a flood, and we are drowning.

Faded charm

I used to watch her like she was a star,
her every word a catalyst for change,
her every move a lesson in power.
Shalini –
her name whispered with reverence,
her presence a force
I thought I could never be.

But now,
her charm has faded,
the shimmer dulled,
and I see her for what she is –
just a woman with polished words
and empty promises.
Her speeches,
her plans,
they're all talk.
Clever, but hollow.

I don't want clever any more.
I don't want speeches.
I don't want the cool, calculated finesse
of someone who never bleeds,
never truly feels the force of a fight.

I want something more,
I want fire,
I want action,
I want to go into battle.
The kind that rips through the air
and leaves no room for doubt.

I want a storm, not a breeze,
a roar, not a whisper.

Her calm, her careful control,
it's not enough for me now.
I need to feel it, the heat, the rage,
the pounding heart of justice
that isn't quiet, that isn't measured,
that doesn't wait for permission.

I think of the women from my past and present.
Jhano tried, but her hands were tied,
my mother had a choice but stayed silent.
I am no sheep.
It's not enough to blindly follow.
I want more.

I want to break the ground.
I want to tear down everything she built with words
and rebuild it with fists, with blood, with truth.

Shalini –
you were a dream,
but I'm awake now!
And I need something real.

Unease

I confide in Rama,
the only one I can trust now.
His eyes, like amber flames,
follow me everywhere.
He sleeps at the foot of my bed
like a protector, silent but strong
in this compound of tension and disappointment.
For me he's not a beast
he's a kindred spirit
an angel on earth
and with him I feel *invincible*.

Rama really likes you, says Shalini
her voice light but her eyes uneasy.
He's never been like that with anyone but me.
She tries to shrug it off like it doesn't matter
but I see it, *I feel it*.

She can feel the shift
and she's rattled,
not just by Rama,
by *me*.
How my presence unsettles the peace she's built.
She knows –
she *knows* she can't tame me
like she's tamed the others.

Broken

I sit in their new home,
a small apartment
on a busy street in Pune.
Not quite what they are used to
but more than most could afford here.

My mother –
she looks tired,
talks fast, words stumbling out in panic,
as if saying them quickly
might stop everything from falling apart.

My father –
he drifts in his own sadness.
Melancholy clinging to him like a shadow.

And I –
I can't find it in me to feel for him.
Yet I sit with him, my hand in his,
desperate to feel something, anything.
To forgive.
But the wound is too deep,
the past too loud.

Still, I stay.

She is the one holding him together,
but she's unravelling too.
How the roles have reversed ...

The money from the house, your father's business,
it'll keep us going, she says,
her voice fragile but forced steady.
You don't have to worry about us, Rizu,
you're doing great work.
You're making a difference.
There's no need for you to worry about us.

But how can I not?
I need to make this right,
I need to fix this broken thing I'm staring at.

How can Sonu's life carry on so perfectly
while my parents have become half of who they were.

Riot

We march in silence,
an army of women, fists held high,
banners raised, eyes burning with fire
but with fire we've learned to contain.
Justice for the girl who never made it home!

Shalini leads, head high, her voice clear,
like a bell ringing over the crowd.
Peaceful, she says. *We protest with dignity.*
We show power through silence.
Rama leads the pack,
another symbol of ferocity kept in check.
We don't need to break things,
to break down systems, she tells us.
But I feel something bubbling in me,
rising like a storm beneath my skin.

We pass the alley where she died,
her blood still staining the concrete,
and I can't keep quiet.
Is this justice? I whisper to the girls around me.
Is this really making a difference?
Does silence honour her life?
My voice shakes as the crowd hums along,
but not loud enough,
not enough to shatter walls.

The police stand watching,
their batons at the ready,
smirking, waiting for us to slip,
waiting for the disruption in our demeanour.

I grip my stick,
feel the pulse of the crowd beneath my feet,
feel the eyes of the women behind me,
their pain mirrored in mine.

This is where Shalini's peaceful protest ends.

I raise my voice,
Justice! Now!
How long do we wait?
The chanting grows louder, fiercer.
Do we stand here, quiet and small,
while they kill us in classrooms,
while they spill our blood in the streets?

NO! the crowd shouts back.

And then
I RUN.

I run through the streets, roaring to the heavens.
Rama right by my side,
our feet pound like thunder on the ground.
I swing my stick, the first window shatters,
glass exploding like the anger in my chest.

The riot begins with my name.

Running through the streets . . .

The girls follow, some hesitating at first,
some running with me without a second thought,
because deep down they feel it too,
this hunger to be heard.

Shalini turns, eyes wide,
the peaceful protest now flames in the wind,
her banner still in hand,
but the roar has swallowed it whole.

She grabs me and pulls me back.
What have you done, Rizu?
Her voice harsh like she's trying to rein in the tiger
that's no longer by her side.

What has silence given us?
What has calm brought to our doors?
Broken bodies, that's what –
another woman killed.

This isn't how we fight, Shalini says,
her voice firm but wavering.
This isn't how we win.

I disagree, I say. *Look around you.*
We take in the shattered glass,
the women whose voices
finally match the rage in their hearts,

knowing,

sometimes you have to tear things down
before you can build them back up again.

Sometimes, Shalini, I say,
you have to run through the streets and roar.

Estrangement

My mother's voice sounds
more faded each time we speak.
Shalini told me what's happening with you.

Oh, are you two best buds now?
Failing to hide the irritation in my voice.

She's worried about you.
We both are.
This isn't you, Rizu –

Isn't it? I thought I was born of fire –

You are, but this isn't the only way to burn.
A slow, steady flame can lead hundreds out of the dark,
but a raging fire just causes destruction.

I knew you wouldn't understand, Ma.
You said yourself you didn't have the guts to answer the call.
Well, I have, and this is my calling.
I finally see it.

You're going to get into trouble.
You'll hurt more than you'll save.
I'm worried for you, Rizu.

To make a change, Ma, you have to rage.
The time for quiet protests is gone –
there are girls to save, to get justice for,
and I'm going to do it, on my own terms.

I can't stand by and watch you ruin your life, Rizu.

Then don't.
The line goes quiet.
Goodbye, Ma.

A coup

Phoolan tells me, *Be patient.*
Annika tells me, *Shalini knows best.*
Sampat says, *Be grateful.*
And Leela – Leela and I no longer speak.

But I ask you,
how many of you have really seen justice play out?

It works, Phoolan says.
Shalini's methods are the right way.

Are they? I look to Jacintha. *What justice did you really get?*

My case went to trial, she answers.

And? I push, because we all know the truth.
Nothing will happen to him.
You know this better than I do.
We have to fight like they fight.
They use violence because it's the only language they know.
Eye for an eye.

I take a breath.

What's the point of all this training?
What's the point in learning how to punch,
to kick and fight, when we don't use our strength?
I'm tired.
Months spent following this so-called warrior woman.
Years before that seeing her on the news, in the papers,
seeing her get revenge, justice.

I thought she was some kind of superhero.
Aren't superheroes supposed to change the world?

The girls are quiet.
Too scared to agree openly,
but their silence gives me confidence to keep going.

Then why haven't things changed?
Why are we still waiting?
I'll tell you why.
Because she's a fraud.
You all told me yourselves,
your perpetrators still walk free.
Annika, Sampat – yours got a short sentence.
Leela, a sham trial.
Phoolan, nothing.
Are you seriously telling me that you're happy with that?

No, of course not, Phoolan admits,
but change takes time.

You don't believe that.
I see the hurt in your eyes when
you talk about what happened to you, Phoolan.

'No one warned me,' you said.
'No one warned me my husband would enter at night,
that my voice would shake and my body freeze from fright.
No one warned me that my pleading would amuse him,
laughter spilling from lips as he grabbed my hips and bit.
No one warned me he would drag me back towards the bed
as I tried desperately to flee. Falling to my knees, I screamed,
surprised by his weight. No one warned me that the memory
of that blood-soaked night would never be forgotten,

the pain of each thrust, his breath, hot.
No one warned me.
No one taught me.
No one helped me
No one saved me.'

I look at her.

Those are your words, Phoolan, yours.
'No one saved me.'
And she didn't, did she?
She didn't save you, not really.

I take her hands in mine.
She should have marched into that man's house,
dragged him out and tortured him like he tortured you.
That is justice.
Do you hear me?
You do to them what they did to you.
It's the only way.

And in that moment I see it,
I see their eyes light up,
I see them hunger for more,
But Ma tells us . . . Sampat begins.

Ma tells you nothing.
It's all a game for her.
It's about the media,
about fame, not us.
Even Rama sees through it.

So what are we supposed to do?

Come with me, I say.
Fight with me.
Let's leave this place.
Start again somewhere new,
fight for real justice,
my way.

I can see them thinking,
Would it work?
Could we break away?
What are you scared of? I ask.

Annika looks at the other girls.
Security. She gives us everything.

We can figure it out.
I take in their faces.
Doubt threatening to overtake.
Trust me.
What is it you said to me, Annika?
Don't let fear dictate what you do.
We are smart and strong and resourceful.

The silence is unsettling but I keep going.

Together we can do anything.
Think about it, but you don't have long.
I am done being quiet.
I am done being obedient,
standing in police stations,
nodding behind Shalini.

It's difficult being quiet, I think,
when quiet is a mouse
and I have the mouth of a lion.

We're in, they say.

We run

It's the dead of night
the world is still
and the moon hangs low
watching us pack
keeping our secret.

We gather our things in silence.
Me, Phoolan, Sampat, Annika and Jacintha.
Barely a whisper passes between us
each movement careful, deliberate,
the sound of rebellion's breath.

Leela watches us.
You're making a huge mistake.

I wish you were coming with us,
I say, my last attempt to win her over,
the distance between us
that took so long to close,
stretched once more.

I catch Annika's eye
her hands shaking as she closes her bag
but in the dark, we all shake
not from fear
but from something deeper
something raw –
freedom calling,
justice gnawing.

Shalini's words
her warning,
fading like smoke.

Rama follows
his eyes glowing
his quiet steps behind mine.
He sensed it too,
the pull of the wild,
the call of the unknown –
he belongs to me now.

We move like shadows, feet light on the earth.
Shalini's home once felt like a fortress,
now just walls behind us.
The air beyond them full of promise.

No more standing behind banners
no more quiet marches
when our hearts scream for more.
This isn't just about leaving a place
it's about leaving a way of life
a way of being told to wait, to be patient.

As we run, the stars seem brighter
the road longer, but ours.
I feel Rama at my heels, his breath hot,
his growl soft like a promise.
Together we'll find our own kind of justice
not in quiet steps but in a roar of our own making.

I lead them,
their trust weighing on my shoulders,
but I know they feel what I feel.
The itch for something real
something violent
something that doesn't ask for permission.

We aren't warriors in training any more –
no more waiting, no more holding back.
We are an earthquake.
We are the force that cracks the ground
and the world is not ready.

SIX

Rebirth

As the group stops for sleep
Rizu takes a walk
down to the forbidden banks
of the Chambal River.

She takes off her clothes
and walks into the water.
She shivers –
the water is colder than expected.

She kneels on the riverbed
feels the earth give beneath her knees
feels it sink between her toes
rise up and surround her.
No one swims here
no one would dare.
The curse, they say,
the curse.

Rizu lies back
lets herself be carried
she is weightless
allowing herself to be taken by the river.

Take me somewhere else,
somewhere new, *Rizu whispers*,
I dare you.

She lets the water work its way around her
she lets it seep into her skin
and nourish her.

She hears Draupadi laugh.
I'm going to make you a thing of legend.
I'm going to make a goddess out of you,
give you the powers of revenge.
Let's conjure a storm
let's unleash havoc
let's knock these self-made gods
off their self-made thrones.
Forget ripples
let's create a wave so high
and so wide
they are drowned by their egos,
the lies they tell themselves.
See us rise instead.

Rizu sinks under the flowing river
eyes closed
and when she opens them
she sees Kali, Durga, Draupadi
and experiences a feeling she has never felt before.
A surge of power,
of magic.
She feels the power of every goddess
and every warrior woman
that came before her.

Her body bends in the water.
It pulses and tingles.
She's pulled under
deeper and deeper
until every last breath escapes from her lungs
and when it seems
like she is no more

*she floats to the surface
gasping for air.*

*Rebirthed
and ready.*

Power

I stand, and the earth trembles beneath me,
its pulse in time with my own.
I am the river now,
its waters, its weight, its fury
all flowing through my veins.
I feel it in my bones,
a thrum that hums of power,
of revenge long overdue.

Draupadi's laughter rings in my ears,
it is a reckoning, a blaze of light that tears the sky wide open.
Kali's wrath is a fire in my chest,
burning with a force that could consume the world.

She is in my blood,
I have drunk her rage,
I have swallowed her fire.
Now, I stand taller than ever before,
my spine straight as the sword in my hand,
my eyes aflame with the fire I've inherited.

These self-made gods,
their thrones are fragile,
their power an illusion spun from lies.
I will shatter their masks,
break their crowns with the weight
of a thousand storms.

They thought me soft,
a thing to be broken.
Now, they will see what I am made of.
Now, they will feel the weight of my rage,
the fire in my blood.
I was born from their cruelty,
I growl, my voice a promise,
and now I rise from it
a goddess forged in blood and flame.

I will tear down their false altars,
turn their empires to ash.
There is no place for weakness in me now,
they will see me for what I am –
a goddess walking this earth,
a woman made of rage and fire,
a force that will not be ignored.

They will bend.
Or they will burn.

Rizu's Army

We see it

Since the night we left,
we have seen it.
A new thing in her –
a magic of sorts,
sparkling like a thread of gold.
It radiates,
rising from her skin like smoke.
We see it.

She carries it in her bones,
this fire, this power
that was born long before her
and will live long after.
We see it.

She speaks and the wind listens.
She moves and the earth stirs beneath her feet.
Her eyes blaze like a star reborn,
and we cannot help but follow.
We see it.

With Rama by her side
she is no ordinary girl,
but a force of nature,
we feel it in our blood,
in the air between us,
the fire she's sparked within us.
We see it.

We see it
and we are ready,
whatever she asks,
whatever she does,
we stand with her,
a leader of a different kind –
a goddess reborn
and *they will* see it.

Vengeance

I thought my transformation
would have me running home,
to tear Sonu apart,
but instead, I wait.
We build.
We train
my way –
a new method.

We hide in the darkness,
we strike when they least expect it,
we are gone before they can roar.

There's plenty more to turn to ash, I say,
and self-made gods to topple from their self-made thrones
and from the parched earth something better will rise
something new and fair, somewhere everyone can thrive.
This is our quest . . .
This is how we rise . . .
This is how we roar . . .
Say it, I demand.
This is our new mantra.
You need to learn it,
breathe it,
dream it,
feel its fire in your bones
till it sets your soul ablaze.

The girls repeat my words,
voices vibrating in the air.
It's euphoric.

This is our quest . . .
This is how we rise . . .
This is how we ROAR!!!
they scream.
Rama growls,
our fury rising.

Unstoppable.

I rise

Month one

I left under the moon, silent, determined,
with the girls close behind.
No fear, just fire in our veins.
We struck, the first blow quick,
a house burned,
a message left in ash.

Already they whisper my name,
Rizu –
with the pulse of every woman
who has ever been silenced.

The first village was easy,
Annika lit the match,
righting the wrongs of her past.
No longer a victim,
she howled to the moon,
and roared for more.

We run from place to place,
hiding in ravines,
the forests,
hunting for our food,
living off the land.

Villagers speak my name in hushed tones,
as if it were a chant carried on the wind.
I am the promise of something greater,
the goddess they never expected.

Little girls watch as I pass
their eyes wide
as if I were a myth come to life.
They want to be me.
They want to be more
than what they've been sold.

Month two

More girls come out.
Too many to count.
They've heard the stories,
they want to join the fight,
they look at me and see
something they seek to be
something fierce
something untouchable.
Steadily my army grows.

I tell them,
We're here to tear the system down,
to build something new from the ruins.
This is our quest . . .
This is how we rise . . .
This is how we ROAR!!!

Sampat's village was next
and when her abusers stepped out,
she danced in the light of the flames.

Month three

The law is on my trail,
but the people – they see me as salvation.
Wanted by the police,
but needed by the powerless.

Girls from the slums, from the fields,
from nowhere – they find me.
They join me,
wanting to be part of the revolution,
to take back what's theirs.
We train in secret,
striking fast,
disappearing faster.

Jacintha, with her fists like storms,
her strength shocking even her.
We unleash her fury
and with it she finds her power
a force unlike any other
getting the justice she finally deserves.

Month four

I walk out in front,
my feet in the dust,
the girls marching behind,
a rising tide.

I hear their pain
and guide them through it.
Not with softness
but with the strength of a goddess,
the fierceness of the earth's roar.

Rama never leaves my side.
He knows what I am,
what I've become.
I can feel it in his gaze –
he is a part of me now,
my companion, my mirror.

Month five

The law shouts louder,
but the people are louder still.
They say I'm their saviour,
the one who will break their chains.
We hit harder now –
those who think they can control us,
we remind them, they can't.

My army is growing.
The girls are finding their power
and it's more than any of us imagined.

Phoolan wanted a revenge of a different kind.
So, we tied up her abuser
and those who silenced her,
did to them what they did to her
and took everything they had.

We are gone before they can roar.
We are gone before they can catch us.
Light in the darkness,
a streak of fire between this land
and their fears.

The damage we do
shocks some of the girls,
but I remind them,
destruction is necessary,
more than necessary,
it is *essential*
and in the silence between roars,
I almost believe it.

Month six

An article in the paper
opens my eyes to an opportunity.
Naresh and Kareena Jain . . .
Reading their names makes me bristle.
. . . parents of the beautiful socialite Sonu Jain,
will host a lavish, star-studded party
celebrating twenty years of marriage
at The Plaza this month.

Everyone will be out,
the precious little gated community
empty for the evening.
This is my chance.

I am ready,
ready to return,
to face a world that shamed me,
to make it bow before me.

It is my turn now...

Back where we started

I stand looking at the house.
It's so quiet,
not a soul in sight.
Crickets providing a soundtrack to the night.
The night hot and sticky,
the air dry, the wind warm.
It's the height of summer
just before the rains . . .

Sonu

Ashes of regret

Farooq, we need to go back to the house.
I've forgotten my make-up bag.

Of course, maam.

Farooq takes the next turning towards home.
Before we reach the gates
we see the flames
and smell the smoke.

Before I can scream,
I see her,
in the shadows,
but clear as day.
She's watching the flames
as I watch her.

I stand frozen
as the flames devour my home.
Rizu dances in the firelight.
I knew this day would come.

I've seen the news of Rizu's rage.
Righting the wrongs with fury in her eyes,
and now, it's my turn.
I thought I had time,
time to make amends
but time is a liar.

The heat of the flames is nothing
compared to the burn inside me.
I started a fire long before this one,
not with my hands
but with the weight of my words –
I called her a witch,
spat accusations laced with anger
and watched as it spiralled.
A wildfire of whispers and rage,
and it swallowed everything.
Jaya's death the final cruel note.

Guilt engulfs me,
a suffocating cloak
each flicker of fire a reminder
of my part in this tragedy,
all the ruins I've sown.

As the walls of my home collapse
so does the version of me that lived within them.
The girl who hid behind hurt,
who let jealousy speak for her.

In the glow of destruction
I'm breaking apart
piece by piece.

And as the fire swallows my home,
and with it my past,
something else rises in its place.
A vow, a reckoning.

I will do better,
I will change.

Because regret doesn't arrive all at once.
It creeps in –
clinging to the corners of your mind,
and if you don't face it,
it will start to hollow you out.

It's a death of sorts
of fear and hate,
of the ignorance I once clung to,
of the lies I told.

And in the embers
I find something I didn't expect –
a glimmer of rebirth.

The house is gone
but from its ashes
I will build something new,
something stronger, something true.

And maybe one day,
something worthy of forgiveness.

They made me what I am!
I hear her scream to the moon
and turn
running and leaping
tripping and tearing
away from the heat of the flames
and into the heat of the night.

I fall

Month seven

Once, my name was carved into the air,
whispered in fear, shouted in hope.
A ghost, a myth, a living legend.
I was their anchor, their goddess.

But now, doubt creeps in.
Some whisper rebellion,
others question my path.
My army now restless.
They say destruction isn't what they sought.
Their path wavers,
and so does my grip.

The hunt goes on,
but my army, no longer fierce,
flickers like a dying flame.
Some still cling to my name,
believing in the justice I promised,
but the roar is quieter now.

I try to hold on
but I feel they are slipping through my fingers.

Month eight

Tragedy has struck.
Rama is injured.

We have fled to safety,
but his wounds are deep,
his strength draining with every breath.

There was a fierce struggle in the heart of our last mission.
The self-made gods fought back,
desperate, and amid the chaos,
Rama fell.
A bullet found him,
tearing through the night,
and though we escaped,
we couldn't escape the price.

I hold him in my arms,
his powerful body weakening,
the light in his eyes dimming.
His roar once thunderous, now a rasp.
I whisper to him, *Please stay, you can't leave,*
who will walk beside me? Who will protect us?

But even a goddess's words can't keep him here.
With one final breath

he is   gone.

The girls watch,
their eyes filled with anger and grief.
Rama was our strength, our protector,
the embodiment of our power,
my power.

Now he lies, cold and still,
and their eyes turn to me,
whispers of blame in the air.

They see my decisions,
my relentless push for destruction,
as the cause of this fall.

Perhaps they are right.
Perhaps my path has led us here.

But even as doubt erodes my heart,
I must stand tall.
I am Rizu,
and gods do not falter.

I rise above their accusations,
even as they waver,
even as some turn away,
I cannot,
I will not show weakness.
I must embody the strength we've lost.

Month nine

Faith in me declines.
My leadership decaying,
as my army dwindles.

The law still hunts us
but we are ghosts
of what we once were.

Month ten

The world talks about me,
but they've twisted my story.
Criminal, vigilante, terrorist,

to them I am a villain,
not a goddess reborn,
no respect for the crown I carry.

My army, now a scattered few,
their trust in me waning.

I press on,
the fractures becoming visible,
trying to be the leader they need,
but I fear I'm losing –
losing myself.

Month eleven

I stand at the brink,
once unstoppable,
now I stumble.
I raise my hand
but fewer follow.

Month twelve

A year.
I am still here.
Barely.
Almost alone,
fighting to keep control.
Though my army is gone,
there are a few that still call my name,
but they are faint, distant.

I catch my reflection in a still pool of water.
Once hating what was on the outside,
the mask I wore to survive,
now,
despising what's within.
The face staring back at me
is twisted by regret,
by the shame of all I've done.

And then,
I see her – Jaya's reflection,
her eyes filled with quiet disappointment
a reminder of what I was supposed to be,
of the justice I promised her.
Her gaze pierces through me
showing me what I've become.

A surge of anger rises
as I call out to Jhano,
I answered your call,
now you answer mine!
I need you, my voice small,
I don't know what I'm doing any more.
I thrash at the water
desperate to shatter the image
to erase the truth staring back at me.
But the ripples only distort it,
the reflection always returns.
I can't escape it –
Rizu, no longer a goddess,
just a girl who has lost her way.

A Stranger

Revenge

For weeks I've tracked her steps
waiting for this moment
justice at last
to end this girl
this terror
this destructive devil.

She's no goddess, no reincarnation,
no divine blood courses through her veins.
I must finish what she started,
end her as she ended me,
destroying my life
robbing me of my livelihood
my money, my pride.

From a distance, I watch
as Rizu and her crew rest,
seeking refuge in the shade,
waiting for the sun to fade.

Sweat runs down my spine,
my heart races.

Crouched and hidden
between rocks in the ravine
I sit and wait,
gun in hand
trembling,
I take aim.

Shooting once,
twice,
three times
to make sure
this devil, this bandit, is no more.

The first bullet for the money stolen
the second for my father's disgrace
the third for the honour my family lost.

I watch Rizu fall,
her body still,
blood running into the earth.

I watch as her life
slips from her lips.
I smile,
vengeance tastes sweet.
I throw the gun.
For my family, I whisper,
and run.

Between life and death

What is this place?

I stand somewhere between here and there
at the edge of everything
where sky meets a void
where silence sings
between breaths, between heartbeats
between what was, is and could be.

I'm floating,
no –
falling –
a ghost in the in-between.

My fingers stretch to grasp at –
something
but the ground beneath me
the space around me,
there's nothing holding my hands
or beneath my feet –
is this the place where life and death meet?

In the empty space I see a figure approaching.
God's a woman! A laugh erupts from my throat,
I knew it!
But, as she comes closer
I recognize a familiar face.
You again, I say, smiling. *Jhano*.

It's me again, she says softly.

Am I dead? I ask.

That's up to you, she says.
There's a sadness behind her eyes.
I recognize it, it reminds me of my mother.

Did I do it right? My calling?
I ask like an eager child needing praise.

It's not quite what I was expecting, she sighs.

I'm fighting fire with fire, just like you said,
I reply, feeling my body tense under her judgement.

Is that what I said?
Her voice hard, but she smiles.
Come, walk with me.

A room of mirrors awaits.
Hundreds of versions of me
staring back, from past, present and the future.

What is this? I ask,
frightened of my own reflection,
of what might be reflected back at me.

It's the mirror you've never dared look into.
But it's time, Rizu.

I feel choked with emotion.
Time for what?

*Time to choose
between rage and reason,
between storms and clear skies.*

*I don't want to look, I can't.
Fear takes hold of my throat.
I can't look at what I've become.
My voice, barely a breath.
Just tell me what to do.*

*I'm not the answer, Rizu,
just the truth you're too afraid to speak.*

I look into the mirrors
at what lies beyond the glass.
The air around us ripples
as my past comes alive.
A flash of memories,
a cruel rewind,
I see myself, young and carefree,
before the mask, before the pain.

Tears roll down my cheeks as images change
and a mask is applied,
still young, but lost,
a darkness settling inside.

The film that plays next
a harsh reminder of the not-so-distant past –
the accusations, the destruction,
I feel myself rise, the anger inside,
the injustice of it all.
I was right, I say. *To do what I did.
Jaya. It was all for Jaya.*

Keep watching, she says,
holding my arm, keeping me rooted
so I can't run from this place.
I relive my time with Shalini,
frustration festering in my bones.
But as life replays itself, I see it differently somehow.
Her approach steady and strong,
my approach like shattered glass.

My crew, the ones I swore to lead.
This is our quest . . . this is how we rise . . . this is how we roar . . .
I shouted, a righteous call,
but all I see before me are broken bodies,
burning buildings, children crying.
Was this justice? Was this my path?
For everything I touched to turn to ash?
Nothing was rebuilt, nothing fair, nothing new,
just destruction and chaos.

That's enough, I say.
I don't want to watch any more.
My chest aches, I turn away,
but the mirrors surround me,
my life continues to play out,
there's no escape.

You can't hide from this, Rizu,
she says. Her voice a summons.

A lump forms in my throat. *I didn't mean . . .*

No more lies, no need to fight.
You thought your roar was to be a raging fire,
but fires destroy, leaving nothing living in their wake.
And now, here you stand between life and death,
rage or reason, to shatter or soothe.
The choice, Rizu, is not about the past,
it's about what comes next . . .

She steps closer, her presence warm.
You were loud, Rizu, you roared,
but there are stronger ways to make your mark.
Violence, it's a fleeting flame.
True justice, well, that's quieter, harder to claim.

My heart pounds in my chest
I feel small and raw
like I'm standing naked before the truth.
Jhano doesn't blame or accuse
she offers me something more –
a chance to choose.

Do you want to live, Rizu?
Do you want another try?
To roar again, but differently this time,
to build rather than break
to heal rather than rage?

I look at the memories swirling around me,
my fists unclench
and my fingers unfurl.
I thought I had to burn the world
in order to rebuild
but now I see something different.

I want to fight. But not like this.
Not the way I've been. My anger
has been leading my quest,
but it hasn't healed, it hasn't helped.
Maybe there's another way,
one that isn't fire, ruin and rage.

Jhano smiles. *Then, that is your choice.*
The void trembles, and the mirrors turn to silver dust.
I blink and the world comes rushing back in.
I feel my breath, the pain of the wounds,
but my body is real, I gasp and taste the air.

The line between life and death now sealed,
I choose to walk a different path,
no more fires, no more screams.
There are stronger ways to roar,
ways that don't leave destruction in their wake.
This is the choice I promise to make.

SEVEN

Redemption

She came back from the dead
with whispers in her head
a new way to be
a new path to tread.

A spell in hospital
treating her wounds
a miracle she survived
now bound to her room.

Armed guards at the door
the most wanted woman
is wanted no more.

Captured for her crimes
once healed
will serve her time.

They roar

Each night I hear them,
the women,
the forgotten ones,
beating fists against iron,
they roar.

Women the world tried to smother,
rotting in this cage,
no sky,
just stone and steel,
the smell of sweat,
a darkness that chokes every breath,
they roar.

This place is hell,
not the fire and brimstone kind,
the kind where hope decays slowly,
where time stretches into eternity,
they roar.

They don't care about our stories here.
We are numbers,
our names lost in a system long ago.
But the walls whisper to me,
remind me of who I was,
because even in the darkness,
we still dream,
the roar we make,
it's not just made of pain,
it's an echo of the lives we claim,
the stories lost and stolen.

Time moves slowly in here,
it twists and turns,
every day a blur.
The guards don't care,
walking past our cells like we're already dead,
like our bodies are just a shell,
but I can't let them win,
this place can't take everything,
my freedom, my time, *yes*,
but not my roar,
that's mine,
that's ours,
the one thing we own.

So, every night when I hear them,
I join them in their fight,
my fists clenched,
hands shaking, voice cracking,
I roar into the night,

because even in the darkness,
I have to believe there's light.

A visitor

The door opens, and there she stands,
Shalini.
I'm caught off guard,
it's been over a year.
The space between us had widened
yet here she is standing like a ghost
from a life I thought I'd buried.

Shalini, no longer the same woman,
she's made her way into parliament now.
I can't help but mock.
Parliament. So, you've traded the streets for suits,
sitting with the rich –
how's that working out for you?

But Shalini doesn't flinch.
Her voice steady and clear,
looking at me like she still knows me,
knows what I'm really saying
beneath the bite of my words.

Don't confuse the path with the cause, she says.
The people seeking help are everywhere,
in the halls
on the streets
in the villages
and every space in between.

I cross my arms, the words stirring something in me
I don't want to acknowledge.
It's easier to hold on to my grudge,
to keep my disappointment neat and justified.

But then she exhales, her voice softer this time.
I should have helped you.
I should have fought the Jains.
I shouldn't have let fear dictate
who is worthy of my help.
She hesitates, then meets my gaze.
I'm sorry.
I promise to do better.

I want to dismiss them,
to remind her that words aren't enough –
but haven't I spent all this time
searching for something other than rage?

I lean back, studying her.
Strength isn't always about being loud
or being visible or being the one on the front line,
I say.
I mean, if you're tearing something down,
you must be ready to build something beautiful in its place.
A woman far wiser than me told me that.

Shalini tilts her head, a glimmer of recognition in her eyes.
Hmm. I wonder who that could have been,
she says with a knowing smile.

We sit in the quiet, still wary, still bruised,
but there's a subtle change.
Not surrender, not forgetting –
but an understanding.

And in that understanding
a new kind of power
a different kind of fight.

Bad news

The letter comes
folded heavy with silence,
words that fall like stones.

My father is gone.

I read and the world blurs.
The edges of everything soften.
I never thought he could break,
but in the stillness of the cell
I feel it,
the weight of his absence,
the intensity of grief,
and the unspoken question –

If I had forgiven him,
could I have saved him?

Building bridges

The phone rings.
My mother's voice,
soft as a prayer,
weakened by the burden of time.

Rizu? Is that you?
The words hang between us,
the gap of a year,
of anger and distance,
now consumed by grief.

He couldn't take what he'd done,
it ate away at him –
this was the only way he could find peace.

We speak of him.
Husband, father,
a man we've both lost.
No answers come,
only the shared ache,
an ache that now binds
what was once broken.

We cry together.
Separate but close.
Two hearts shattered
by the same goodbye.

Freedom

Where are you taking me?
As they drag me from my cell.

Why aren't you talking to me?
As her grip clamps my wrist.

Tell me what's going on!
As she shoves me before a desk.

Sign these papers,
barks another voice.

What are they?

Your release papers.

What? Is this some kind of joke?

We don't joke.
Sign them or stay.

I stare at the form,
the words a blur of legal jargon.
It doesn't matter.
One thing pierces through the haze –

I am free.

Saving grace

As I leave
There is one person waiting for me –
Sonu.

We stare at each other,
across the tarmac,
an ocean between us.
She pauses before walking over.
I search for signs of ego,
the Sonu who dripped in glitter and gold,
so shiny and bold.

But this Sonu is different,
more shy than shallow
she bites her lip, nerves kicking in.

I look at her and something clicks.
Is this you?
Are you the reason I'm free?

Yes, she says. *I hired a lawyer,*
the best in the country. It's my way of saying sorry –

I cut her off.
I don't want your guilt money to walk free,
not when there are women in there, Sonu,
women with less than me
women who have been left to rot
women who deserve the world.
I feel their pain ripple through my core.

How can I walk out
while they stay locked away?

Because you can do more, she says.
You can do more, out here,
than you could ever do in there.
You're not just a fighter, Rizu,
you're a leader, a flame,
but you can't lead from a cage.

I don't want your charity, I say, my voice strained.

This wasn't charity, she says.
You wouldn't even have been in there if it wasn't for me.
I owe you this.
Please accept it.
Now you're out, you can work towards
changing this whole system, you can set others free.
Out here, Rizu, you can roar louder than those walls will allow.

A silence hangs heavy
all that's been and done
all that can't be erased
laid out for us to see.

If you can believe it, I've changed, she declares,
her voice quivering. *I swear I'm not that girl any more.*

Is that so? I say through a smirk, not convinced.

I've had a rebirth. Like you, I died and came back.
She looks at me, eyes wide, like she's seen God.

My laughter is real now,
the first to escape my belly in months.
I should thank her for it.
I don't think your spiritual rebirth
is the same as taking three bullets, Sonu.

Of course, you're right. She searches for words.
I'm not asking you to understand
or forgive me, but I'm not who I used to be,
I'm different now. She looks at me like she believes it.

What does that even mean, when you're still
shackled to the family that tried to kill me,
you are the reason Jaya is dead,
you're still daddy's girl, I say with a sneer.

No, she says, shaking her head, *I've given up that life,*
started another, I've shed that skin.
She pauses for a moment.
I . . . I volunteer now.

What do you want? A medal?
Well done, Sonu, no longer ruining lives.

She takes a deep inhale.
I deserve that. But believe me, Rizu, I've seen the light,
I'm trying to make amends. I've gone out into the slums,
I'm working with my hands, I'm trying to build something new.

I laugh again and see her eyes fall.
Regret clings to her,
tighter than any gold necklace ever could.
I'm building a school, she finally says.

For Dalit children. I'm going to call it 'Jaya's'.

Are you joking? I say with a burn.
You're naming a school after the girl who died because of you.

Yes, she says, her voice small.
I have to make things right.
For her, for you.

For me? I spit.
My voice echoes off the iron gates.
You think I want your privilege?
You think I need your guilt-stained gold?
Let me guess, you're using daddy's money?

She's quiet for a moment.
If it's being used for good, what harm can it do?
I know my family has used money to ruin a lot of lives
so for once let it be used for good.

She reaches across to me, takes my hands in hers.
Give me a chance, let me make this right.
Rizu, I swear, this isn't about me any more.
I've seen what power does. I've felt its weight.
I want to heal, I want to help,
and you, you're the key to that gate.

What do you mean? I ask.

I want you to help me with the school,
to run it with me, build more, in every state.

I look at her,
really look at her for the first time
in a long time.
Maybe, I think, maybe she's not the same girl,
the one who threw me to the wolves.
Maybe she's been through her own hell too.
Maybe rebirth isn't a lie,
maybe it's something you also have to fight for.

All right, I say, *but this isn't the end, Sonu.*
This isn't forgiveness, it's . . .
the beginning of something new,
and we have to fight,
for every woman in this hellhole to get help.

She nods
and I feel something between us shift
not gone, but different.

Maybe we both needed this to happen, I say.
Maybe life needed to take us on this path.
We both needed to change.
To do better, to be better.
We both had to die and come back.

Freedom

It is true what they say.
Money makes the world go round.
The rich and powerful
make their own rules
when money changes between the right hands.

The taste of freedom is bitter in my mouth
but the air outside the iron walls is sweet.
My privilege feels heavy.
Like a lead weight round my neck
it chokes.

To cut the chain
is to make good on my promise.
To be the change

but still roar for more.

Closure

My first visit out of here
can be to one family only –
not my own
but Jaya's.
They deserve to know the truth,
they deserve to have closure,
they cannot go on believing their daughter ran away.

As I approach her village
my heart starts to thrum
and as I see her house
my legs start to shake.
How do you begin to tell a family
their child was murdered?
How do you begin to explain that?
How do you begin to tell them that you are to blame,
that her life was sacrificed for yours?

I take a deep breath and walk towards the house.
Children play outside,
I watch a woman heat water on a stove.

Kumari?

The woman looks up,
she has Jaya's eyes.
She stands, wipes her hands.
Who's asking? she says.

My name is Rizu Malhotra, I begin.

And as I recount the events, she is silent.
It's only when I am done that she holds her chest
like she's trying to stop her heart from falling out
and roars to the high heavens.

She roars and roars.

She roars for her daughter's life
she roars for the lies
she roars for the injustice
each one creating earthquakes beneath my feet.

And what now?
There will be no justice
there never is for people like us! she cries.
My daughter's life meant nothing to you
your life more precious than hers.

It wasn't, I say. *It isn't*, I correct myself.

And your father?
Will he pay for this?
Or will you keep him safe?

My father took his own life,
I tell her. *He couldn't cope with what he did.*

Well, that's something, she says.
Not justice, but something.

I feel winded but understand
why she must hit hard with her words,
knowing I would feel the same.

I tell her the name of the witch doctor.
Lalu, I say, *he's already been reported,*
an arrest was made yesterday.
She looks at me
like she doesn't hold out much hope for a conviction.
Arrests are made and men are always released.
We serve and serve and serve,
put on this earth to serve the rich
and there is no way of escaping the cycle.
If we try, even if we raise our voice just a little,
we are beaten down.
Witch-hunting never went away, she continues,
it just operates under many different names.

I'm silent.
It seems there are no words left to say,
no words to make it right.

Did she fight at least,
did she fight for her life?

She did, I say,
till her last breath.

That's something, she says.

Giving voice

I stand on a makeshift stage
hands sweating, heart racing
my eyes scan faces in the crowd
taking in all the young girls.

I take a deep breath,
there's an ache in my chest
but I stand strong and firm
ready to speak a truth
that's been caged for too long.

I never thought I'd stand here.
Not like this,
certainly not with Sonu.
There's a ripple of recognition
for our personal story in the crowd.
We're here today to open a school for girls,
girls who have been told 'you're less',
who've been taught to bow their heads
before they ever knew to stand tall.

The school will be led by Leela –
my good friend – as its headteacher.
I smile at her, grateful we could mend what I broke.
Leela's strength and wisdom are unshakable.
She will lead this school with the unwavering light of a guiding star,
nurturing a generation of girls who will grow
with the unyielding roots of ancient trees,
their spirits unbreakable,
their voices a chorus that will echo through time.

I once thought the world was a box,
wrapped in silk, a child of privilege,
dressed in luxury, fed on lies.
*But this – **this** – is where I was meant to be.*
Not gilded in gold, but carved from iron,
tempered in fire, reborn in ash.

Jaya's School for Girls is named after my friend.
She worked for my family and we became close,
well, as close as we were allowed to become.
So, here at this school, we will aim
to close that divide, to empower,
to show the world that caste division has no place here,
everyone can rise and become whoever they choose to be.
Girls like you were born to lead.

By now you know my story.
The accusations, the gang,
the violence, my incarceration.
For a long time, I thought that was
the end of my story.
Standing here I realize
it was just the beginning.

Today we open our doors
for every girl who has been told 'you can't'
for every girl who's ever been crushed
under the weight of caste, class, expectations, of fear.
This school is not just made of walls and books
it is a promise. A promise that no girl
will ever swallow her voice again
that no girl will ever have to watch
the world from behind bars
whether they be made of iron, or fear, or shame.

I stand here, not as the girl I was
but the woman I have become.
I stand here for Jaya and
for every girl here today.
I stand here for you.

I pause, the audience erupts in applause.
I'm breathing hard, looking out to the crowd
my breath catching in my throat when I see them.
I swallow, a tear falling down my cheek.

There – my mother
drowned in grief so deep and dark it swallowed her whole.
I watched her disappear day by day
but today she stands tall, no longer a ghost
but a woman who learned to roar again.
She raised me even when it hurt.
Her heart heavy with loss
but she found the light again
in herself
in me.

Today she smiles like she's never known sorrow
her strength quiet but unshakable.
She taught me what it means to survive
to love when it feels impossible.
She showed me that even in the darkest night
we can be our own stars.

And then, there's Shalini,
fierce as fire, a true warrior in this world.
Took me in when I was broken, angry and lost.
She didn't tell me to soften, to shrink,
she taught me to fight.

Once standing on the edge of lawlessness
but now standing in parliament.
She is proof that change is not a dream
but a revolution in motion.
And now she echoes names in halls
that were not meant for them.
She taught me that power doesn't wear a mask of violence,
it wields a pen.

And finally, there's Jhano.
I pause, seeing her once more.
Jhano. The ghost of the woman
who's walked beside me
through fire, through death,
whispered to me in dreams,
reminded me that my roots run deep
from a line of warriors.
She stands smiling at me now
her spirit at peace
her strength in my bones.

I wouldn't be here without them
these women who shaped me
who carved their name into my story
with every tear, every battle, every sacrifice.

I take a deep breath,
cheeks glistening,
eyes locking on my mother,
on Shalini, on Jhano
their smiles wide
their pride shining as brightly as the sun.

Thank you, I whisper.
Thank you.

EPILOGUE

The warrior's roar

She was the rich girl
the ordinary girl
overlooked and silent
but something stirred –
a fire
a fight.

In moments of darkness
she found her way to the light
no longer a warrior with fists
not a soldier with a sword
but a rebel with a heart.

Her battle cry changed
from a scream to destroy
a legacy of ash
to a whisper that moved mountains.

She learned to roar
not with violence
not with vengeance
but with the steady sound of strength
the soft echo of empathy.
Strength isn't the blade that cuts the skin
but a hand that reaches in
to lift, to hold, to build again.

They said she'd fallen
that her fire had flickered out
but death doesn't always mean defeat.
She came back, not as the girl who had lost her way
but as someone new
someone stronger.

Onwards she goes
what she'll do next, who really knows
but the ripples she makes
are now circles of change
no longer waves of destruction.
Even the smallest steps
she now sees
can shift a world
and give a people a new way to be.

Now look at you,
standing still
wondering if you have the will.
But inside you there's a weapon
a spark, a fire, a sound,

harness its strength,
don't wait, don't hide, don't fear the fight.
Let it rise from the deepest part of you,
let it echo around the earth
a sound that moves the stars,
and shakes the ground beneath your feet.

So,
Rise, my warriors, rise,
create your ripples
let them spread, let them soar
and change the world forevermore,

because
even the smallest ripple can become a wave
and every whisper a
roar.

A Note from the Author

Hey there,

First off, thank you for picking up this book. Seriously, it means a lot. There were moments when I wasn't sure I'd ever finish it. It's been a tough one – rewritten, torn apart and pieced back together more times than I can count. But in the summer of 2024, I finally found Rizu's voice, and here we are.

I wanted to share a bit about how this story came to be, because it wasn't just an idea that popped into my head – it was something I had to dig deep to find. And that digging took two years of research, conversations with incredible people, and a whole lot of listening and learning.

A few years ago, I came across a UN report that stopped me in my tracks. It talked about the rise of witch-hunting in India, and I was horrified. According to India's National Crime Records Bureau, more than 2,500 acts of violence linked to witch-hunting had been recorded since 2000. And the actual number? Probably way higher, because most of these crimes – especially those against Dalit women – go unreported. I couldn't wrap my head round it. How was this still happening?

I started reading everything I could find – articles, interviews, reports. What shocked me most was that almost all the victims were Dalit (lower caste) women. Crimes like these rarely targeted the upper caste. It became clear that this wasn't just about superstition – it was about deep-rooted caste prejudice, patriarchy and government apathy. I had always thought of witch trials as something out of history books. But this is happening now.

That led me to research India's past witch trials, and I found out about the 1792 Santhal witch trials – the earliest recorded in India. The Santhal people, an Adivasi (Indigenous) community in the Chotanagpur region, believed witches were responsible for disease and bad luck. The solution? Eliminating them.

Around the same time, I became obsessed with the story of Sampat Pal and her Gulabi Gang – this badass group of women in bright pink (gulabi) saris who take on corrupt cops, abusive husbands and anyone else standing in the way of justice. Armed with pink-painted bamboo sticks, they fight for women who have no one else to turn to. Their leader, Sampat Pal, was married at twelve, had her first child at fifteen, and never learned to read or write, but she still managed to empower thousands of women.

Then there was Phoolan Devi – India's 'Bandit Queen'. Forced into marriage at ten, she was abused, then turned into an outlaw and later became a Member of Parliament before being assassinated in 2001. She was seen by many as a reincarnation of the warrior goddess Durga. I figured if Shalini was a character inspired by Sampat Pal, then Rizu was meant to embody Phoolan Devi.

At some point, all these stories started connecting in my head, and I knew I had to write something. But before I could start, I had to understand the reality. So I dived into research – not just reading, but talking to people who had lived through this. I spoke with activists and organisations like the International Dalit Solidarity Network in the UK. They were my first point of contact when I started thinking about this book.

This is probably a good place to give a quick crash course on India's caste system. It's an ancient social hierarchy that's been around for over 3,000 years. It dictates people's place in society based on birth – upper castes hold privilege while lower castes, especially Dalits, have faced systemic oppression for centuries, and even though discrimination based on caste has been legally abolished, it still dictates social realities in many places. If you've read my other books, you know I'm always drawn to stories about underdogs – about people fighting back against the odds. So, originally, Rizu was going to be a Dalit girl accused of being a witch. But then, an important question was asked: why me? As someone from an upper-caste Sikh background, was it my story to tell? The women I was working with early in the process, activists here in the UK and India, thought not. The more I listened, the more I realized they were right. The answer was no.

So I changed course. Instead of telling a Dalit girl's story, I wrote Rizu as someone from an upper-caste, privileged background. While witch-hunting is rare in upper-caste communities (less than one per cent of cases), it still happens. And, more importantly, it allowed me to shine a light on the realities of Dalit women without speaking over their voices.

The Crucible played a big role in shaping this book, too. It's one of my all-time favourite plays, and its themes – mob mentality, mass hysteria and how society turns on its own – still feel painfully relevant today.

Finally, I wanted this story to feel truly epic, drawing from the tradition of grand tales where our heroes rise from unexpected places and are elevated to a near-mystical status. They celebrate extraordinary deeds and reflect the values and ideals of a society while weaving in elements of mythology. Introducing magical realism elements was essential to capturing that epic quality, making the narrative feel extraordinary. I wanted Rizu to lose herself completely – to dismantle everything she had ever known about herself and the world around her.

This is why the book took four years to write – it started as one thing, lost itself, found its way back, and became something new. I had to unlearn, to step away from ideas I was attached to and start afresh. And honestly?

It was the best thing that could have happened. It forced me to grow, to listen and to tell the story in a way that felt right.

I hope this book resonates with you. It has been one of the hardest things I've ever written, but also one of the most meaningful. Whether you see yourself as one of the quiet ones or not, this book is for you. May it help you find light in the dark and your voice through the chaos.

With love,
Manjeet

Acknowledgements

This story found its shape
thanks to many hands –
the ones who cheered, who questioned,
who helped me understand.

Carmen McCullough, Joseph Coelho, Sandip Sidhu, Meena Varma, Gauri Banu, Ruth Prasad, Shreeta Shah, Emily Smyth, Janene Spencer, Felicity Trew, Caroline Sheldon, Claire Wilson, Kushiaania, Binita Naik, Lottie Chesterman, Michael Bedo, Nina Douglas, Lucy Doncaster, George Maudsley, Eleanor Updegraff and Mollie Schofield.

© Sam Irons

Manjeet Mann is a multi-award-winning author, playwright, screenwriter and actress. Her debut YA novel, *Run Rebel*, was shortlisted for the Carnegie Medal and won the CILIP Carnegie Shadowers' Choice Award, along with several other accolades. Her second novel, *The Crossing*, won the Costa Children's Book Award, among other honours, and was also shortlisted for the Carnegie Medal, the Waterstones Children's Book Prize and the YA Book Award. Manjeet also writes picture books, including *Small's Big Dream*, which won the Readers' Choice Award at the Diverse Book Awards. She adapted *Run Rebel* for the stage with Pilot Theatre, earning Best Production at the Off West End Stage Awards. Manjeet lives in Scotland.